CRUSH

A SWEET FULL-BODIED QUEER ROMANCE

L. DREAMER

Copyright © 2022 by L. Dreamer

All rights reserved.

No part of this book may be reproduced in any form or by any electronic or mechanical means, including information storage and retrieval systems, without written permission from the author, except for the use of brief quotations in a book review.

Edited by: Cate Ryan

To all my trans brothers who deserve a happy ending.

ACKNOWLEDGMENTS

I'd like to thank my beta readers, Mildred, Ange, Andy, Crystal, Teddy and Chloe. You all are amazing and this book wouldn't be half as good without your time and care. Thank you.

And to Charlie and Jayden, you guys inspire me every day and I'm so glad we found each other!

PROLOGUE

Mia watched her husband's casket as it was lowered into the ground. Her mind desperately searched for something else to focus on. It landed on the idiom *six feet under*. Did they really bury people six feet deep?

A voice to her left, hoarse with tears and timid with circumstance, interrupted her absurdly timed curiosity. "I'm so sorry, Mia." She turned her head and reached a hand out to Margaret, her sister-in-law, who took it and squeezed. "I can't believe he's gone."

"Me either," Mia whispered. Her musings were abandoned as anger, hot and sharp, sliced through her chest. Her husband did not belong in that casket. He should be there, with her, celebrating their fifteenth wedding anniversary and their winery's first harvest. She wanted to break out of Margaret's grasp and run—run to her husband's casket, back to their home in San Francisco, all the way to that fucking bar in Monterrey where they met.

As quickly as the anger came, it gave way to staggering sorrow. Her mind raced as it added up all the what-should-have-beens and what-will-never-bes. She dropped her chin to her chest and took in two big open-mouthed breaths. "Mia? Do you need to sit down?"

I need my husband back. She shook her head. "No, I'll be okay." The lie felt heavy on her tongue.

PART 1: DORMANCY

1

Cal drove his 1979 Chevy C10 truck through the gates of Torwood Winery, careful not to kick up too much dust as he passed workers maintaining a drainage ditch. When he came upon the ranch house, he saw a woman on horseback riding toward him. The woman watched him intently as he pulled up as close to the edge of the drive as he could, mindful of the horse. He got out of his truck and was surprised to see she'd come around the back and was waiting for him next to the tailgate.

"Hello. Are you here for the vineyard manager interview?" she asked, not unkindly, but not friendly or welcoming either.

He smiled, slipped the sunglasses off his face, and tilted his head up as he came closer. "Yes. My name is Cal Sanders."

"I'm Mia Torwood." She studied him, her honey brown eyes giving nothing away. He knew he looked young. Perhaps too young to be applying for a job at a winery that size. But at the age of thirty-five, he had the degree and decades of experience already.

Finally, she nodded. "Drive down to the barn. Ask for Jose. I'll see you down there in a few minutes, Mr. Sanders."

"Okay," he called out to her back as she had already heeled her horse's flank and was heading down the way she came.

Cal was already nervous, and the cool reception did nothing to quell it. Perhaps that was the way the woman was. All business. "All right Cal, let's do this," he said, giving himself a little pep talk as he pulled back onto the dirt road and down the hill.

The property was beautiful. Gorgeous old oak trees lined the road until it opened up to the vineyard itself. Rows upon rows of grape plants lie dormant, resembling weathered scarecrows with their gnarled limbs spread along the fruiting wires. There were two main lots on the south facing slopes, one for the Grenache crop and the other for the syrah.

As he came around a bend, the building with the green roof came into view and he slowed to take it in. It looked like it was original to the property because it was built of wood, but very well-maintained with a fresh coat of paint. The ground floor had big roll-up doors, and Cal could see that it housed a lot of the equipment used to maintain the vineyard. He saw windows on the top floor and a set of exterior steps leading up to a tiny balcony and a single door. The vineyard definitely had charm in the way it held on to its original heritage, and Cal couldn't help but picture himself working on it.

He pulled into a spot and got out. He immediately spotted an older man wearing a battered straw hat, hands on hips, staring at a compost spreader. He was short and round and sported a thin goatee. His skin was dark and weathered from years laboring in the sun. Cal approached him and gave him a tentative grin. The man waved him over with a smile that reached all the way to the crinkled corners of his soft, dark eyes.

"You must be Cal Sanders," the man said as he pulled off his calf-skin glove to shake Cal's hand. "I'm Jose Montoya."

"Nice to meet you, Mr. Montoya." Cal gestured to the spreader. "We have these on our vineyard. They are good, but finicky after they've been sitting for a while."

"Yeah, we only bought these last year. The chain keeps seizing."

Cal was already rolling up his sleeves. "Mind if I take a look?"

Jose nodded as a corner of his mouth slid up and he stepped aside. "Be my guest."

Cal bent down and studied the chain. "Even after lubricating these suckers, they still like to be taken off and adjusted. Even if you had them adjusted right before putting them up for the season."

"Finicky is right. Let me go get my bigger toolbox. We'll talk while we work, if that's okay?" Jose's smile was wide, and Cal instantly took a liking to the man. "I can't think of a better way to see if you'll be my replacement than to work alongside you for a bit."

They had the chain off by the time Mia rode up. She looked from Cal to Jose, her brow furrowed slightly. "Jose?"

"Hello, Mrs. Torwood. Cal offered to help fix the spreader. I promise, I am actually interviewing him as we work." Cal expected a lighthearted grin or laugh from Jose as he told her, but his face stayed serious, his tone deferring.

She nodded, and after another long look at Cal, dismounted. "After you two have finished with the spreader, come up to my office. We'll go on a tour of the grounds together."

"Yes, ma'am," Jose said with an obedient nod. All business, indeed.

Cal watched her walk her horse around the corner and waited another few long seconds. "I didn't get you in trouble, did I? Jumping right in to help?"

Jose blew out a breath and raised his hand dismissively. "No, no trouble. Mrs. Torwood is just like that. She's also not happy that I've finally decided to retire. I've put it off for a few years to help her... and her husband... keep the winery running, but my wife, she's been very patient, you know..."

"If you don't mind me asking, where is Mr. Torwood?"

"He passed away almost a year and a half ago. Right out in the rows during their first harvest. It was..." Jose's voice fell away as he shook his head. His eyes fell to his boots for a moment before he looked back up to Cal. "It's why I put off retiring for another year. To help Mrs. Torwood."

Cal nodded slowly as he felt a twinge in his chest. *Jesus, how awful.*

"Yeah, the winery... It was pretty obvious that it was her husband's dream, you know? I'm not sure why she's staying, to be honest. But she's never talked about selling it. Not once."

"Is she pretty involved in the day-to-day?" If Cal did get the job, he wondered how much he'd be working with her. A lot of the new winery owners only wanted their name on the bottle and left nearly everything up to their managers—from pruning procedures, growth maintenance, even what varieties were planted.

"Not so much. She is very on top of the finances though, I can tell you that." He let out a chuckle. "You'll have to come very prepared whenever you ask for new equipment, personnel, materials."

"Of course. That makes sense." It really did. His own

family's winery wasn't big, and every expense had to be worth it.

"I've had a few interviewees balk," Jose said with a slow shake of his head. "There are a lot of egos out there—and a lot of sexism."

Cal was well aware of the sexism in the wine industry. Before he'd transitioned, he'd experienced it firsthand. During his transition, he learned how transphobic it was too. That was part of the reason he wanted to branch out on his own. His family was whole-heartedly supportive, but some of his family's business associates were not. Moving from the insular central valley winery community to the much bigger central coast offered him a fresh start presenting as the man he'd always been inside.

"Well, I'm confident in my abilities, but I also know running a successful winery takes a lot of cooperation."

"And hands!" Jose laughed as he slid the newly adjusted chain in place. He powered up the spreader and ran it for a few moments before shutting it off. He stuck his hand out again and Cal shook it. "Well done, Cal!"

After Jose directed a worker where to start the compost spreader, he gestured for Cal to follow him. They made their way up the external set of stairs on the other side of the large building. Jose stopped them on the landing. "I already like you, Cal, but it is up to Mrs. Torwood who she ultimately hires. A word of advice? Don't treat her like she's new to this." Cal nodded in understanding and Jose gave him a lopsided grin as he opened the door.

The office was expansive, almost dwarfing the L-shaped desk that sat about ten feet from the door. Behind it was a line of file cabinets with a large, framed picture of Mia and her husband walking the rows during veraison when the grapes began turning color. He was handsome, tall, and slender and all his focus was on Mia. Cal felt another dull pang in his chest when he compared the carefree smile the woman had in the picture to the contemplative frown she now had as she studied something on her laptop.

Mia's 'all business' demeanor shifted in Cal's mind. He didn't know her at all, but what he saw now was a woman who was perhaps still grieving, not to mention under a considerable amount of stress. Cal knew firsthand how difficult it was to run a winery. Triple the size of his family's and only one cycle removed from new ownership? Not to mention having to hire a new manager? No wonder she seemed serious and solemn.

Jose stood a few feet from the desk but didn't speak. Cal stood next to him, silent as well. After a few more seconds, Mia looked up. "Ready to tour the vineyard, Mr. Sanders?"

Cal smiled and ducked his head in the affirmative. "Yes, of course. And you can call me Cal." He tacked on after a beat. Hearing Mr. Sanders gave him a thrill of affirmation, but it was also how everyone referred to John Sanders, his dad.

She halted her ascent from her seat for a fraction of a second, as if the request gave her pause. She finished standing and gave Cal a polite smile before turning to Jose. "We'll take the Mule. It'll be faster than walking."

"Of course, Mrs. Torwood," Jose said. He made his way out the door and back down the stairs, leaving Cal alone with Mia.

Mia leaned forward and put her forearms on her desk. "So, what do you know about the history of this winery?"

Cal almost smiled at the question. She wanted to see if he did his homework. "It was started by the Giambi family in the late 1930s. They were one of the first wineries in California to blend syrah and Grenache to great effect; their vintages have been consistent award winners."

The subtle raise of Mia's right eyebrow let Cal know he'd passed the first test of the interview, and he breathed a little easier as she asked her next question. "Your resumé says this will be your first managerial job. What makes you think you're qualified to run my vineyard?"

"I have a degree in viticulture and enology from Fresno State and I've worked alongside my father for nearly twenty years. I know the entire process from planting canes to going to pressing." He paused when her expression remained impassive. "I love the science of growing wine grapes, but also the magic of it. Cutting that first bunch off right after veraison, tasting the literal fruit of your labor..." He let his words drift off, afraid of sounding a bit too impassioned. He was pleased to see that Mrs. Torwood's eyebrows had lifted slightly in apparent interest, however.

"Wouldn't you be the one to take over your family's vineyard in the future?"

"My dad, sister, and I have discussed that—they know I don't want to live in the central valley. When the time comes, my sister and her husband will run it." Cal knew it made his father sad that he would not take it over, but he understood Cal's desire for a fresh start, away from the small-minded town.

"Understandable. It's like a furnace in the summer, isn't it?" Mia's smile transformed her face, and Cal was enchanted by the drastic change. It was like getting a glimpse of the carefree woman in the portrait.

Cal returned the smile and nodded. "It can get pretty unbearable. It's very hard work to protect the fruit from the sun."

"So, do you produce chardonnay, merlot, or cabernet?"

Cal wasn't surprised Mia knew the three main wines produced in the valley. "Cabernet, though I did convince my father to plant a Merlot test vineyard last year."

Mia nodded, and Cal could have sworn he saw the corner of her lips curl up slightly. "Well, I'm sure you're aware that we are continuing the Giambi's legacy by producing syrah."

"That makes sense. Why reinvent the wheel?" Cal reasoned.

"Right. It didn't make any sense cost-wise either. Tom and I... we want—wanted—to make things easy on ourselves the first few years." Her stumble on the past tense and pained look in her eyes set off an ache in Cal's heart. Mia's sadness was still very close to the surface. He'd witnessed that in his own father when his mother passed away from a brain aneurysm five years ago. Mia recovered quickly, though, and smiled warmly. "We were so grateful that Jose stayed on for as long as he did. He's an excellent manager and teacher."

Cal was taken aback by her effusive praise. He had a feeling she didn't dole it out often. He also took it as a barometer of how big the shoes were that needed to be filled. No doubt the intention of her words. The fact that Jose was already ready to endorse him filled him with an immediate sense of pride and confidence.

"Ready for that tour?" Mia stood and Cal followed her out to the stairs.

As if on cue, Jose pulled up with the four-seater Mule and waved them over. "Mr. Sanders—I mean Cal—go ahead and sit up with Jose." Mia gestured to the front passenger seat. The gentleman in Cal wanted to argue, but he realized she probably had a reason for him to be up front.

They toured the vineyard for a good hour, Jose stopping

periodically to check the dormant canes. He peppered Cal with questions asking what his techniques were, how he would deal with pests, rot, freeze threats. Cal explained what he did on his family's vineyard but also included how the valley and coast were different and how he'd adjust his approach.

He, in turn, asked about the last couple of harvests and any issues they'd come up against and how they'd solved them. All the while, he kept an eye on Mia through the rearview mirror, trying to gauge her reaction to his questions and answers. Her expression was mostly unreadable, but she did interject with questions and answers of her own. Jose said she wasn't involved in the day-to-day, but she obviously knew what was happening at her winery.

The actual wine making part of the property was housed in a large, sleek brick building that was painted a subtle brown but had that same green on the metal roof as the old, wooden barn. Mia let them into what Cal saw was the grape testing room. There were several stations, and the equipment looked state of the art. As they walked through, Cal noticed a man at the opposite end watching them intently.

"What do you think, Cal?" Mia asked. He turned to her, embarrassed at not hearing the question. "I know, we've thrown a lot at you," Mia said with a patient smile. "I was talking about playing around with the destemming process, maybe making a couple of different varieties when blending it with the Grenache."

The question felt like a test, and he treated it as such. "I imagine it depends on how much help you can get during fermentation. Syrah takes quite a bit of management, especially when you go the partial destemming option."

Mia nodded, and Jose gave him an approving wink. Seemed he'd passed.

There was a new voice, and they all looked toward it. "I tried to get the Giambi's to work in a couple of different varieties of the blend in the past. Glad Mrs. Torwood is willing to try new things." It was the man who had been watching them.

Jose gestured to the man as he came up to stand next to Cal. "This is Samuel Hastings. He's our winemaker, but he's here pretty much every day, helping out with whatever needs to be done. He's been here almost as long as I have. He knows his stuff."

Samuel ducked his head as his lips lifted into a half-smile. His eyes went to Mia before moving to Cal. "You interviewing for the manager's job take it? You look a little young." He chuckled as he put out his hand.

Cal internally rolled his eyes. "I'm older than I look," he said as he shook Samuel's hand. Cal's grip was firm, but Samuel returned it two-fold. Cal matched his grip for an instant before releasing his hand. Whereas he took an instant liking to Jose, Samuel was a harder read. He wasn't sure what to make of him.

"Cal, if you wouldn't mind following me back up to the office so we can wrap up." Mia's voice cut into Cal's thoughts, and he looked at her and nodded.

"Of course." He turned to Samuel. "It was nice to meet you."

"Nice to meet you too," he said, drawing out the words in an almost mocking tone. Or was it Cal's imagination? He shrugged it off as he followed Mia.

"I hope to see you soon, Cal," Jose called out as he headed back to the equipment building. Cal smiled at the man and made his way up the stairs behind Mia.

Once they were back at her desk, Mia told him to have a seat. She pulled out a folder from a short stack, opened it, and scanned it, giving Cal a moment to study her. She was a few inches shorter than he was with dark chestnut hair and eyes the color of wildflower honey. She had a smattering of freckles across her nose that made it hard to guess her age, but he thought she might be at least five years older than he was, if not more.

"I imagine you have an idea what salary you're looking for?" Mia looked up quickly, and her eyes flashed wider for a second when they caught Cal's.

Cal blinked, embarrassed he'd been caught staring. "Oh, uh, yes. I'm just starting out, so I'm still feeling out numbers…"

She nodded and grabbed a notepad, scribbled something in it, tore the page out, folded it, and pushed it in front of Cal. He looked at her and then at the paper and picked it up. He opened it and schooled his features when he saw the number. It seemed like a lot, but he knew it was on the low end of a manager's salary for a vineyard that size, but truth be told, he would be very comfortable with the amount. He found himself really hoping he would get the job. It would be the perfect experience for him.

He pushed it back and nodded with a grin. "That would be fine."

She returned his grin with her own subdued smile and stood, holding her hand out. "I'll be in touch then, Cal." He stood slowly and shook it. Once she released his hand, she gave him another polite smile. "Have a good rest of your afternoon."

He sidestepped the chair and pushed it back where it had been. "Thanks for your time, Mrs. Torwood."

As Cal trotted down the stairs, he looked up over what he could see of the vineyard. With the exception of Samuel, he had a really good feeling about the place. He could picture himself working there. It would be a challenge for sure, but he'd be coming in right at pruning time and would immediately be able to make his mark on the place. The size was a bit daunting, but he knew that only meant it would take more time and manpower.

He was excited to potentially put his education and experience to work. He even looked forward to working with the enigmatic Mia Torwood if she saw fit to hire him.

MIA PULLED HER ROBE TIGHTER AS SHE WALKED TO THE OPEN window and closed it, sad that the weather had become too cold to leave it open. She loved the scent of damp earth once the evening dew set in. She couldn't count how many times she'd fallen asleep to the sound of brittle oak leaves brushing against one another in the gentle breeze.

She made her way to the bed, removing her robe as she went and tossing it on the chair in the corner. She climbed under the duvet and reached for the book she'd started the night before, a crime-thriller series she'd been working through since that summer. But her mind kept drifting to Cal Sanders.

Mia didn't want to hire a new vineyard manager. She'd even offered Jose a substantial raise, hoping to at least get him for another year, but it was not to be. She liked and trusted Jose and now she would be starting all over with someone new.

Her first impression of Sanders was that he was too young to be applying for the vineyard managing job, but he had a degree and he'd grown up on a winery. And, he was older than he looked. During the course of their interview, she never felt like he saw her as anyone other than the owner. And he got the all important endorsement from Jose.

Mia had always been supportive of her husband's endeavors, but when he came home, excited about a winery he'd toured and fell in love with, Mia was skeptical. When he started talking about moving to the central coast full-time to make wine, Mia thought he was joking.

They had recently finished renovating their three-story Victorian that sat in the heart of the NoPa district in San Francisco and Mia had loved every moment of it. But Tom had been convincing in his enthusiasm. *"You can have a horse, Mia, and the house, it's beautiful with just enough work to be done for you to make it your own. Imagine how romantic it would be, to own a winery."*

It took a year for them to move because Mia had wanted to do all the renovations first. During that time, she began to see the allure of the property. Not for its status as a long-running winery, but for its subtle beauty and the solitude she found. When she'd purchased Lucas, a retired race-horse, she thought she might finally be acclimating to life on the central coast.

But then Tom had died suddenly of a heart attack on the first day of their first harvest. In the midst of her shock and grief, she'd learned that a series of questionable investments Tom had made had depleted their accounts and the winery was their only real asset. So, she was stuck living out her dead husband's dream, all the while doing her best to make sure it didn't become her nightmare.

Everything depended on the winery being successful. She didn't have the time or the luxury to be angry at Tom for keeping their financial situation from her. She simply dusted off her dormant accounting skills and got to work. Then came Jose's announcement that he was finally retiring and that created a whole new set of worries. Who could she get to replace the man, who for all intents and purposes, was irreplaceable?

When she couldn't convince Jose to stay, she'd asked if Samuel, his right-hand man, could take over, but Jose said he wasn't a good leader. Exasperated, she begged Jose to put together an ad for the job and to help her interview people for it.

She'd learned quickly in the first couple of interviews that, like every other male-dominated profession, sexism and misogyny ran rampant. Cal seemed different from the rest. He treated her like she actually owned the winery, not Jose.

She stared down at her book, suddenly not in the mood to read. She set it over on the nightstand and let out a jaw-cracking yawn. Might as well go to bed early. She had plenty to do the next day. Her first order of business would be calling Cal and offering him the job.

2

Cal slowed as he turned into the drive that led to Torwood Winery. Instead of nerves stemming from an impending interview this time, he was brimming with excitement. He had his whole life in the back of his truck and his whole future right in front of him.

Even though Cal's father knew he had interviewed for a job that would take him away from the family vineyard, he had worried about telling him the news he'd gotten the job. But like always, his father had put Cal at ease. *"I wouldn't have suggested you branch out on your own if I wasn't prepared to have you leave. I'll miss you, but I'm so damn proud of you, son. And I know Mom is smiling down, proud of you too."*

He hadn't realized his eyes had filled with tears until the cool breeze from the open window chilled his wet cheeks. He brushed them off quickly and shook his head with an amused chuckle. He'd always been a crier.

He was greeted by Mrs. Torwood once again as he pulled into the driveway in front of the house. She wasn't on horseback this time and she welcomed him with a warm smile as she came up to the driver's side window. "Morning, Cal.

Mind if I jump in with you? I'll show you that apartment I told you about, see if it'll work for you."

"Sure," Cal said, surprised at the warmer reception he was receiving. He watched her as she went around the front of his truck and climbed into the passenger seat.

When she'd offered him the job, she had told him about the apartment on the other side of her office, saying it was his if he wanted it. He knew that during certain parts of the growing season, he'd need to be there around the clock, so it definitely made sense to stay on the property. The idea of not having to look for a place to live and pay rent was also very appealing.

"So, this barn was the first building on the property. Even before the house. The family lived on this second floor while the house was being built," Mia said, her keen interest apparent. "Then once the house was finished, they split the top floor into the apartment and office." Cal nodded, impressed with her knowledge of the history of the winery.

After he parked, they got out and Mia led them up the stairs to the landing where he stood a few treads down while she took out her keys and opened the door. "It isn't much, but it is furnished."

"I'm sure it'll work. Thanks for offering it," Cal said. He'd sold a lot of his furniture right after getting the job, intending to buy better stuff once he'd received his first paycheck. Now, he could save it and put more toward a down payment on a house.

It only took him a minute to check out the bedroom, kitchen, small living room and bathroom. "This is perfect," he said with a grin.

"Excellent. Let's go up to my office and get your paperwork filled out and then you can get settled in." Cal nodded and followed her out and down the stairs. As they were walking past the equipment room on the first floor, Jose intercepted them with a wide smile.

"Congratulations, Cal," he said, holding out his hand.

Cal returned his smile as he shook it. "Thanks, Jose. I look forward to you showing me the ropes before you head off into retirement."

"Happy to do it," Jose said before turning to Mia. "I'm confident I'll be leaving you in good hands, Mrs. Torwood."

Mia nodded, smiling cautiously. "I know you'll do your best, Jose. I really appreciate you staying on an extra month." In that moment, it hit Cal how much weight would be on his shoulders. He allowed himself a few seconds of panic, then mentally shook it off. Growing grapes is what he did and had been doing since he was fifteen.

"Okay, last one," Mia said as she handed the form to Cal. He made a show of shaking out his hand, causing Mia to chuckle lightly. As he got to work on it, she refocused her attention on the email she had been composing. But, as she'd been doing over the last twenty minutes, she snuck another glance at him.

She'd already noticed his long, dark lashes and the way he'd chew at his thumbnail in concentration while filling out his tax forms. When he was completing his background check, she was surprised to see a sizable area on the crown of his head where his hair was thinning.

But, as she studied him now, filling out his emergency contact form, she came to the conclusion that even if he were to go bald sooner rather than later, he'd still be quite handsome. *Where did that come from?* She shook her head to clear it of the inappropriate thought and shifted her attention back to her email.

A few moments later, she heard him blow out a short breath. "Okay, all done."

"Great, thank you." She took the form and scanned it, noting that he'd listed his father and sister as emergency contacts. *So, no wife or serious girlfriend—or boyfriend—in the picture.* Was that really the first thing that came to mind? *Get a grip, Mia. What is going on with you?*

"Was there anything else you needed from me?" he asked as he set the pen down and gave her a polite smile.

"No, I think that is it. Why don't you get settled in and then you can track down Jose when you are finished?"

"Sounds good," he said and stood. He was almost to the door when he turned around and fixed Mia with a wide grin. "I'm really looking forward to working with you, Mia."

Mia studied him for a second. She wasn't sure if it was wishful thinking, but she had a good feeling about Cal and what he could bring to the winery. "So am I, Cal."

3

Cal ran his fingers over the knotty wood of the dormant grape vine, searching for the two thickest, strongest branches that would be the base from which the new growth would begin. The process of cutting and removing last year's canes and chutes was time consuming and tedious, but Cal enjoyed the labor. He was outside, in the fresh air, doing something he loved.

He was cognizant of the workers around him in nearby rows, doing the same. His approach to pruning was similar to Jose's, and it only took an hour of demonstrating and shadowing to make sure they were all on the same page as far as technique went.

"Jefe, we are done with this block. Me, Marcos, and the others are moving to the north corner now!" Freddie yelled from the end of the row Cal was working. Cal waved his hand, indicating he'd heard him. He was very thankful that Freddie, Jose's nephew, had stayed on. He was a quick study and never questioned Cal when he did something different from Jose. If he could only get Freddie to call him Cal instead of the Spanish word for boss. It had been a compromise when he refused to call him anything but Mr. Sanders.

"I never seen canes cut that way. You're gonna crowd the buds."

Cal didn't need to turn and look to know who was standing over his shoulder. His technique of picking the two biggest branches, called canes, and tying them horizontally along the fruiting wire was a tried and well tested one. "As you can see, I've added an additional fruiting wire. I've explained this to Mrs. Torwood, and she is in agreement that this type of pruning will add to the fruit yield." Cal stood noting Samuel's pinched expression. He set his jaw and held the taller man's gaze until Samuel looked away to focus on the cane Cal had been tying.

As soon as Cal began passing as the man he'd always known he was, he'd had to get used to asserting himself with men like Samuel. It was exhausting and silly to Cal, but he found it made his life easier in the long run.

"Leaf pruning gonna be a bitch later on. Labor's gonna wash out any higher yield profits."

"Not in my ten years of experience in training canes like this. Mrs. Torwood and Jose were not happy with last year's production. They were both on board when I suggested the change." Cal knew the statement would irk Samuel—who was the winemaker, after all—but it was the truth.

"Well, far be it for me to question something that has already been decided." His tone was light, accompanied by an easy grin, but Cal picked up on the disdain he didn't bother to hide in his eyes.

Samuel was very adept at his job, that much was apparent. He'd been there almost as long as Jose and had been instrumental in some of the award winning vintages when the Giambi's still owned the winery. But Cal guessed there was a good reason why Mrs. Torwood wanted to look outside their current personnel for the vineyard manager job.

"It has been. Also, I could really use your help. Row forty-two hasn't been pruned yet." Cal kept his eyes on Samuel's as he gestured downslope. He didn't look away until he saw the reluctant acquiescence in Samuel's.

"Sure thing." He ripped the gloves out of his back pocket and sauntered down the hill. Cal watched him for another moment before sighing heavily and returning to his work.

He was deep in thought, working away with his pruning shears when he saw a shadow fall over him. He clenched his jaw, ready for another confrontation with Samuel. He turned, shielding his eyes from the sun with a scowl on his face. It immediately fell away. "Mia."

"Hi, I don't mean to interrupt. I wanted to see how you did the pruning. I feel like I don't know a lot about the process. Figured I should."

He'd been there a month and he'd only seen Mia a handful of times, so he was surprised to see her in the rows, asking to learn, no less. "Yes, sure. You want to give it a try?" She nodded eagerly, making Cal grin. "First, you'll need gloves when you are reaching into the old growth. It can tear up your hands." He pulled off his gloves and offered them to her. He half expected her to politely refuse or tell him she'll just watch instead, but she took them without a word and slipped them on.

"How do you know what to cut and what to let grow?" she asked, looking at the tangle of growth.

He handed her the shears and pointed to two long vines on either side of the trunk. "We choose four shoots from last year's growth to tie to the fruiting wire. Those shoots are where this year's shoots will grow from. You want to pick ones closest to the trunk that are fairly thin and pliable." He nodded to the vine he had just started.

"You want me to choose?"

"Sure," Cal said.

She knelt down and studied the vine. "How about these two on this side?" She said, gesturing. Cal nodded and leaned over, pointing where to cut. She brought the shears up and clipped the shoots, then tore the old growth away carefully.

"You don't have to be too gentle. The wire will hold up."

Mia yanked at the growth and it pulled free. She moved to the other side, again looking up at Cal for approval. "Looks good. You're a quick study." He smiled at the pleased look in her eyes.

"Thanks for letting me bug you about teaching me."

She moved on to the next vine and ended up doing three more before looking at her watch from underneath the too-big glove. "I have to get back up to the tasting room, but thanks for the pruning lesson," she said as she pulled the gloves off and gave them back to him.

"It was my pleasure. Feel free to come and help anytime."

Mia's laugh was light as she turned to walk back toward her office. "Will do. It was a nice break from being cooped up inside."

M<small>IA PUSHED AWAY FROM HER DESK AND STRETCHED HER ARMS</small> up over her head. She'd been working for five hours straight on the coming year's budget. She welcomed the mild headache, the slight burning of her eyes. It felt good to put her accounting skills to the test.

She'd always found comfort in the absoluteness of numbers. They were black and white. Plug them into a formula, get results. Numbers were predictable. Far removed from the volatility of life. There were no surprises in numbers. No pain, no sadness, no fear.

She sighed as she swiveled her chair around to look at the portrait of her and Tom. Her husband was a different man once they'd moved to the winery. He had found his passion for life again—something that had been slowly siphoned away in the cut-throat venture capitalist world.

It was like they'd started a whole other life at the vineyard. One that was far removed from the high-stress, high stakes life they'd been caught up in. And then it was over before it really began. Tom had died and had left Mia to navigate this new life all on her own. One she was stuck with now because financially, she was tied to it. And she had no choice but to make it work.

She remembered how she thought Tom had lost his mind when he wanted to take her down the coast to look at a winery for sale. She smiled absently at the memory of listening to him talk about his plans for the winery. How excited he'd been. Now, she was starting their second growing cycle without him, and she still felt like she could be swallowed up by a wave of grief at any given moment.

She wanted to see what Tom saw in the land. What he felt when he was out walking the rows and helping Jose. It was what prompted her to go seek out Cal and get a lesson on pruning. The more she understood about the process of winemaking, the more she thought she could feel a bit of what Tom did.

"Okay, Mia. Another hour and then you can go to bed," she murmured to herself. She shook her mouse to wake up her computer, which had gone to sleep, and cocked her head when she heard the faint sound of a guitar. She looked toward the wall that separated her office from Cal's apartment. She didn't know he played. She didn't really know much about him at all. She concentrated on the notes, trying to place the song. After a moment, though, she gave up. Perhaps she'd ask him when she saw him next.

She had been impressed with Cal so far, a month into his employment. He was extremely knowledgeable, and she could tell he'd been doing a lot of research on growing the hardy syrah grapes. He brought ideas to the table but listened first before speaking and offering his opinions.

Jose had been an excellent, but old school manager. Cal seemed to know the value of keeping some of the older elements of grape growing while introducing more efficient, sustainable methods. And he was passionate about the process. She'd found herself caught up in his enthusiasm and it had taken her by surprise. It had been so long since she had felt anything other than sadness, worry and anger. It was a welcomed change.

PART 2: BUD BREAK

4

"That's annoying." Cal wrapped his towel around his waist and reached up to see if he could tap the recessed bulb in the ceiling to get it to stop flickering. He smiled in triumph when it stayed on but it began flickering again seconds later. "Damn," he mumbled as he stared up at it. He knew it would drive him crazy if he didn't fix it so after he got dressed, he went in search of a replacement bulb.

He found a box of them in the utility closet by the front door, and after grabbing the step stool that was in the kitchen he swapped it out. He frowned when it continued to flicker. "Must be a loose wire up in the box," he said to himself. He walked to the hallway and did a little fist pump when he saw that not only did he have attic access, it had the fold down ladder steps.

He went to his bedroom and flipped the circuit off from the breaker box in his closet and grabbed his headlamp. He then climbed the steps into the attic. He was pleasantly surprised when he peered around and saw it was bigger than he thought it would be. Someone had laid down plywood through the middle, so he didn't have to worry about balancing on the joists.

"Okay, where are you?" He aimed his light in the direction of the bathroom and spotted the junction box that fed power to the can that housed the light. He kneeled down and tested the wires and sure enough he'd found a loose one. He tightened it back down and as he was about to stand up, his light caught on something under the vent that was in the exterior wall.

Mindful of staying on the plywood, he walked over to it and bent down. "What's this?" Covered in a quarter inch of dust was an old, oversized shoebox. Trying his best not to disturb too much of the dust, he opened it slowly and looked inside. Shining his headlamp down, he found about a dozen letters still in their envelopes. He pulled one out and ran his thumb over the faded ink, then he pulled out a few more. They were letters all addressed to a Patricia Giambi from someone named A. Harris.

He squinted at the postmark, trying to see the date, but the glare of his headlamp and the faded ink made it hard to read. One thing was for sure though, that box and those letters had been up there for decades. Intrigued and excited at his find, he put the letters back and gingerly put the top back on the box and picked it up.

After making his way out of the attic, he put the box on the kitchen table and went to check the bathroom light. Relieved that was fixed, he returned to the box. Instead of opening it again, he cleaned it off the best he could, deciding to give it to Mia straight away. He had a feeling she would be very interested in diving into the mystery letters.

He fixed himself a bowl of oatmeal and ate it as he stared at the box. He wondered how the letters had ended up in the attic, all by themselves. Unable to ignore his curiosity, he lifted the lid once more and pulled a letter out.

The postmark on it was from Sweetwater, Texas, February 7th, 1943 and addressed the same as all the others. He flipped it over and although the envelope glue had long lost its adhesive, it didn't look like it had actually ever been opened. There were no tear marks or evidence the letter had even been taken out of its envelope. "Huh." He took out the rest of the letters and arranged them all in chronological order. The last letter was dated July 3rd, 1943.

He didn't feel right actually opening any of them, so he put them back in the box, trying to keep them in order. He put the lid back on the box and finished getting ready for the day.

Ten minutes later, Cal bounded up the set of stairs on the other side of the building that led to Mia's office. Halfway up the stairs, he realized she might not be in yet but figured he could leave it on her desk since she'd given him a key to her office. He let himself in, set the box on her desk, and grabbed a sticky note and pen.

Mia-

Found this box in the attic when I went up there to fix the bathroom light. Might make for some interesting reading.

Cal

He paused for a moment before signing his name, wondering if he should put some sort of closing word like *thanks*, or *Sincerely*. He settled on putting his name and stuck the sticky note to the top of the box. He caught himself smiling when he thought about Mia coming in and seeing the old shoebox full of letters. He hoped that she'd share with him the contents of the letters as well as any context she would be able to find out. He wondered if it would be inappropriate to ask.

He shook his head to chase away those thoughts and focus on the big day of pruning he had ahead of him. It was, after all, what Mia had hired him to do.

MIA EXPERTLY JUGGLED HER MUG OF COFFEE, HER PURSE, AND her messenger bag on one side of her body as she unlocked her office door. She pulled it open and stumbled her way in before the self-close mechanism caught her ankle. "Christ." She huffed out an exasperated laugh and dumped her bags down in her chair and sat her mug on her desk.

"What's this?" she said as she walked around by her chair to read the note. It was written in neat block letters and she smiled unconsciously as she read who it was from. Intrigued, she lifted the note off the box and read it. "Huh." She murmured and pulled the top off the box. Her eyes widened with curiosity as she pulled out an envelope.

"Patricia Giambi." She read aloud, searching her memory for the name. If she remembered correctly, she was the youngest daughter of Paolo and Sophia Giambi, the original owners of the winery. She looked at the name of the sender, but it didn't ring a bell at all. There had been a few different surnames involved in the running of the winery and they'd all been of the husbands of the female side of the Giambi family. Harris was not one of them, though.

She placed the letter back into the box knowing if she opened it, she'd be busy going through them for hours. She set it on the cabinet behind her, powered up her computer, and got to work.

Before Mia had realized it, the morning and part of the afternoon had flown by, and her stomach started to make its displeasure known. She went to grab her purse when her eyes lit upon the box. "Oh, yes, forgot about that," she said as her brain shifted from numbers and her mood lightened. She was very much looking forward to heating up some soup and diving into the letters as she ate.

She grabbed her purse, tucked the box under her arm, and headed out the door and down the stairs. She was at the foot of the stairs when she saw Cal talking to Freddie in front of one of the irrigation tanks. He had on his customary wide-brimmed hat, lined flannel jacket, dark jeans, and a pair of pruning shears in one back pocket and a pair of gloves sticking out of the other one.

She hadn't thought much about his appearance when she'd first interviewed him except to note that he looked a lot younger than he was. He appeared to be barely out of his twenties, even with his neatly trimmed beard and slightly receding hairline. She'd decided it was his eyes that made him look so much younger. They were bright and expressive and framed by longer than average thick, dark lashes.

He was on the shorter side, perhaps no more than three or four inches taller than she was. He had a stocky build but wasn't overweight. He seemed very strong and solid, almost the opposite of Tom who was nearly a foot taller than her and very lanky. She'd joked that if he turned sideways, she could lose him in the rows of vines.

She caught eyes with Cal and gave him a polite smile, leaning into the distraction to derail her train of thought. It was easier to think about Tom without wanting to cry as more time passed, but it felt strange to think of him the same time she thought about Cal. It felt wrong to compare them in any capacity.

"I see you got the box," he said as he walked toward her.

She held it up. "I did. You said you found it in the attic?"

"Yep. I had to get up there to fix a loose wire and saw it

sitting by itself. I'm no expert or anything, but I don't think they've ever been opened. It looks like they were from the forties."

"Really? That's interesting." Mia was already thoroughly intrigued by Cal's find. She couldn't wait to look into the letters. She cocked her head, though, as she looked up at him. "A loose wire? I can have someone look into that, Cal." Although she was glad he'd found the box of letters, she felt bad that he had to climb up to fix something she could have taken care of.

"Oh, it was easy. And I wouldn't have found the box otherwise," he said with a wide smile.

"This is true." She nodded, unable to hold back her own smile. "Thanks again for bringing it to me. I'm off to lunch now, so I'll have a little peek at them."

"You're welcome, Mia. Enjoy your lunch." He tipped his hat and started back toward the rows, leaving Mia alone. She promptly tucked the box back under her arm and made her way to the golf cart she got around in when she wasn't riding Lucas.

Once back at the house, she put some soup on to heat and sat the box down on the kitchen counter. She opened the first letter carefully, noting that Cal was right, it appeared it had never been opened prior to it being sealed.

Dearest Patricia,

Well, I made it to Avenger Field! What a trip it was. If I never see another Greyhound bus, it'll be too soon! Texas is very different from California. For one, it's very flat! And people here really do talk a lot slower!

There are women from all over the country here and our first night in the barracks was a real gas. Our unit was threatened with a reprimand because we kept each other up with all our excitement.

I'm excited for what's to come. The training, the uniforms. Getting to fly the P-51's! I'll write as often as I can, but know that I think about you every day, Patty. Please don't forget about me!

Yours,

Anne

Mia slipped the letter back into its envelope and picked up another one. It had a lot more detail about Anne's daily training and Mia smiled when she read about a flight instructor named Lieutenant Arthur Dimwittle who kept swearing, forgetting he was teaching women.

As she read through the letters, she got a sense that Anne and Patty might have been more than just close friends. Of course, she knew things might have been different all those years ago, but there was a paragraph in the last letter that she read twice.

My dearest Patricia, I'm not sure why I continue to write to you. It is obvious you have forgotten about me. I cannot tell you how much that hurts. Have you found another friend to occupy your time? A beau, perhaps? If that is the case, you have truly broken my heart. All I ask for is a simple note to let me know.

Still Yours,

Anne

Mia put the letter down and stared at it as she finished the rest of her soup. She made a mental note to do a little more digging into who Anne Harris was and what became of her and Patty.

5

The shrill alarm jerked Cal awake, and it took him a second to register what was happening. "Shit, the freeze alarm," he mumbled as he threw off his covers. He grabbed the jeans he'd worn the day before off the back of the chair in his room. He picked up his phone and hit the contact button for Freddie and put him on speaker as he pulled on his boots. "Freeze alarm went off. Call Samuel, Grady, and Guzman," he said and then hung up when he heard Freddie grunt his acknowledgment. He grabbed his gloves and jacket and made his way out the door, bounding down the stairs and heading to the front where the big sliding doors were.

He had the giant fans pulled out and hitched to the Mules by the time Freddie arrived. The rest of the guys arrived a few minutes later and within thirty minutes of the freeze alarm sounding, they had the fans running on the rows.

"Turn on the sprinklers." Cal instructed Grady who nodded and ran off to the irrigation valves.

"It's twenty-nine degrees, Jefe," Freddie said as he came

to stand next to Cal. Cal dipped his head as his lips formed a grim line. He'd had Freddie and the workers mow between the rows to keep the frost line as low as he could, so now it was up to the fans and steady spray of water to keep the new, vulnerable buds from freezing. If they froze, their crop was done.

"Syrahs are hearty. They'll be okay." Samuel looked out over the rows as an almost bored expression settled on his face. "We've never had a wholesale loss due to freeze."

Cal held his tongue. He wasn't going to argue with Samuel. He might just be trying to reassure him, but in the couple of months he's gotten to know Samuel, it was unlikely. The overconfidence rubbed Cal the wrong way, but it was a waste of time to call him out on it.

"We've got it handled here, Samuel. Thanks for your help. Why don't you head home and get some more sleep."

"If you're sure," he said, pulling off his gloves already.

"I'm sure. I'll see you in a few hours." Cal watched him as he began walking backwards to his truck, but something drew his attention over Cal's shoulder and he stopped, heading back toward Cal.

"Mrs. Torwood, good morning." Samuel nearly pushed Cal aside to get to Mia, taking the large carafe and stack of cups out of her hands.

"Thank you, Samuel," she said, letting him unburden her. "I heard the freeze alarm go off and thought I'd bring down some coffee." She reached into her coat pocket and pulled out a jar that looked like it was filled with milk and a handful of sugar packets. "I improvised," she said with a laugh.

Samuel reappeared, holding his hands out once again. "I'll take those too. I pulled out a cart to put everything on."

Mia dropped the packets into his right hand and held the jar out to the left.

He scurried away and Mia turned back to Cal. "What's the temp?"

"Twenty-nine. Fans and water should be enough to keep them from freezing." Cal's eyes went from the rows to Mia. The look of worry was plain and obvious. He gave her a confident smile, trying to channel some of Samuel's bravado. "They *will* keep them from freezing."

"I know the new buds are very fragile. Do you think we should buy more fans? I heard some owners use helicopters..."

Cal shook his head. "The measures we're taking will be sufficient."

Mia looked out over the rows, brows drawn together. "If you're sure. I can't... We can't afford to lose..." Her words trailed off and Cal realized Mia's true level of worry.

"I'm sure. The freeze line is well below the new buds. The water, though it might not be the most cost-effective, is very effective in fighting frost. I'll stay out here and watch everything, I promise."

She opened her mouth to speak, but Samuel came up between them, a cup of coffee in each hand. "Mrs. Torwood. I put in sugar and a little bit of milk. Is that okay?"

Mia stepped back half a step in surprise. "Oh, you didn't have to do that, Samuel. I brought it out for you guys." She took the cup he had held out in front of her though and nodded her thanks.

"There's plenty, Mrs. Torwood. Thank you for bringing it out," Samuel said as he took a sip from the other cup. "I'll keep Mrs. Torwood company if you want to grab yourself a cup."

Cal started toward the cart, but his eyes caught Mia's

and he saw something in them that he recognized. Discomfort. "Nah, I'm good. I'll have some in a bit." He then turned back to address Mia. "Want me to walk you back up to your cart? I'd like to talk to you about an idea I have, if that's okay?"

"Sure. Thank you." Mia nodded and then lifted her cup toward Samuel. "Thanks for the coffee, Samuel."

"I'll be right back." Cal threw over his shoulder as he gestured for Mia to walk in front of him. He swore he could feel Samuel's stare burning into his back.

"Thank you, Cal," Mia said after they were out of hearing range. Cal gave her an understanding smile. He'd had his share of experiences with men like Samuel before coming out and transitioning. "Did you really have an idea you wanted to talk to me about?" Her tone was light and it made him feel good that she seemed to trust him. One of the things he had yet to get used to was women feeling uncomfortable around him when isolated.

"Actually, I do. When I was in school, I did a ton of research on biodynamic farming which is very similar to organic farming. It centers on using biodiversity to enhance crop growth, like varying what is planted and acquiring animals to add in composting options..."

Mia looked up at him with interest. "So, like getting cows? Growing things other than grapes?"

"Well, we wouldn't need to get cows. We had goats on our vineyard and I know how to handle them and care for them. They will help with vegetation management as well. You can rent them out too. Also, if we can get the vineyard certified biodynamic, you can command a higher price for your wine."

"Really? Well, it sounds like quite an investment upfront. But I trust you know what you are doing. I'm gonna put my faith in you," Mia said as the corner of her lips quirked up into a smile. But Cal felt the gravity of her words.

It was a big change he was proposing and to have Mia's trust meant a lot. This was his very first job, after all. But he knew how to grow grapes. It was in his blood. He also had the experience and driving ambition to prove to himself that he could be one of the best vintners in the area. "I won't let you down, Mia."

A ghost of a smile threatened to grow larger, but Mia dipped her head and stepped back. "I'll see you in a few hours, Cal."

THE FREEZE ALARM WENT OFF FOR ANOTHER THREE DAYS straight and each time Mia had brewed a pot of coffee, poured it into the carafe and made her way down to the equipment building. She liked feeling like she was part of the crew as they all stood vigil, making sure the fragile buds didn't freeze.

After the coffee was consumed and the frost threat abated, Cal would walk her to her cart. They would spend a few minutes talking about goats and which crops would put what kind of nutrients back into the soil. She was surprised at how much he knew about farming in general.

She'd been a little disappointed after the first morning had passed without a freeze alarm. Of course, she was relieved, but she missed the camaraderie. So, when she'd parked her cart and headed toward her office, she lingered a bit, hoping to catch Cal.

"Morning, Mia. No overnight freeze."

She turned at the sound of Cal's voice and grinned. "Yes, it was nice to sleep right through to my alarm."

Cal let out a wistful sigh. "I haven't needed an alarm in years. My body just wakes up right before the sun."

"Every time?"

"Every time, unless I'm sick, which is hardly ever." He grinned and knocked on the wooden wheelbarrow handle he happened to be standing next to.

"So, I've been thinking about the goat idea," Mia said.

Cal's grin settled, and he looked at her with keen interest. "Yeah?"

"I think we should do it. There's plenty of room in the barn and they can share the pasture with Lucas. He'd probably enjoy the company."

Cal's eyes brightened. "Yes! I'm sure he would. How do you feel about the companion crops too? We can plant peas and beans. That will help put nitrogen back in the soil."

Caught up in the momentum of Cal's enthusiasm Mia smiled. "It all sounds good, Cal. How about you come up to the office after lunch and we'll get the ball rolling."

"Great. I'll be up there around two?"

Mia nodded. "See you then, Cal."

Cal tipped his hat. "Have a good morning, Mia."

She watched him walk off toward the rows and shook her head, laughing. "Goats? Peas? What am I getting myself into?"

6

Mia set her phone down and put it on speaker as she opened her fridge and grabbed the coffee creamer. "Come on, Lloyd, I know you're up," she mumbled as she poured some into her coffee and stirred it.

Finally, a gravelly voice came on the line. "What's shakin' honey?"

Mia grinned at her best friend's greeting. "Goats."

She sipped her coffee as she waited for Lloyd's reaction. It didn't take long.

"Come again?"

Mia talked to her best friend Lloyd at least three times a week since moving to the central coast. He was her confidant, sounding board, shoulder to cry on. When Tom had died, he'd come down from San Francisco for nearly a month, making sure she ate and slept—which was all she was able to do the first couple of weeks. She didn't know what she'd do without him.

"Cal suggested we make the vineyard more sustainable by turning it into a biodynamic farm. It's basically turning the farm into one living organism. Planting beneficial crops that put nutrients back in the soil, getting some goats for weed clearance and composting material. Everything from pest control to soil deficiencies is all done without any synthetic stuff."

Lloyd hummed in interest. "Sounds expensive. Is it expensive? I don't know anything about farming. But I know I pay a lot more for organic stuff. Is that what you're talking about?"

"More or less. It's a bit of an investment at the start, but it makes sense and it's the direction farming is going. Ironic that it is one of the oldest methods of farming," Mia said, leaning against the counter as she nibbled on a piece of toast.

"And this was Cal's idea, huh?"

Mia dipped her head, smiling down at her shoes at her friend's leading question. Ever since she'd made an off-hand comment about Cal being attractive, Lloyd had been like a dog with a bone about it. It was innocent fun and Mia found she enjoyed the good-natured teasing. It was safe and as Lloyd pointed out gently one night after they'd both drunk about half a bottle of wine, it reminded her she was still a hot-blooded woman with wants and needs.

"It was." She rolled her lips against her teeth to keep from laughing when Lloyd sighed heavily into the phone.

"Is that all you're gonna give me? Is he still teaching you grape growing *techniques*?"

She rolled her eyes at his deliberate enunciation of the last word but decided not to comment. "Lloyd..." she said in warning, letting him know his teasing was coming up to the line where she felt uncomfortable. He acquiesced, immediately apologizing. "Apology accepted," she said with warm affection. "I'm learning a lot. He takes the time to explain so much of the process. Yesterday we walked the syrah lot, and he showed me how he decides on which shoots will be better producers than others."

Lloyd hummed approvingly. "I'm glad he's working out, honey. You deserve to have someone who can help you run that place. How are you doing otherwise?"

"I'm doing okay. Sales from last year's vintage are really steady. Proceeds from the rental house I sold in Lake Tahoe just came in..."

"I asked how *you* are doing," he chastised softly.

She knew what he was asking. So much of her life was wrapped up in the winery though, it was hard to separate the two. She pushed off the counter and took her coffee cup to the sink as she thought about how to answer. "Days are getting easier. Nights are still hard, but not as hard as six months, or even a week ago..." She paused, trying to recall anything else that had happened since they talked last. A wide smile spread across her face when she remembered. "Oh! Cal found some letters in the attic space above the apartment. They seem to be love letters from a woman to one of the Giambi daughters during World War Two. I've been doing some research on them both."

"Oh, that sounds intriguing. A delicious little lesbian mystery!" Lloyd cooed with enthusiasm.

Mia smiled and shook her head. "I'll let you know what I find."

"Please do! Oh, I gotta run, Matthew is here. We're going on a morning run, wish me luck!"

"I should probably wish him luck," Mia teased and laughed again when she heard him gasp in indignation. God, their morning conversations always put her in a good mood for the day.

"I'm coming down there soon, and I want to meet this

Cal. You've been warned. Love you, sis. I'll talk to you in a couple of days."

Mia didn't even try to get a word in before the line went dead. Her cheeks ached from smiling so much during their brief conversation. The smile didn't leave her face either when she remembered she'd be meeting with Cal that morning to go over the details of getting the vineyard certified.

CAL CHECKED HIS FILE FOLDER ONCE MORE BEFORE HE LEFT HIS apartment. He wanted to make sure he had all the information for Mia on biodynamic certification. If she wanted to go that route, it would add a lot to Cal's plate, but he was up to the challenge. It was his idea, after all.

He made his way down his stairs and around the barn to Mia's side as he went over the key points he wanted to make. He bounded up her stairs and gave her office door a cursory knock before opening it. "We still good to meet?"

Mia looked up and blinked at him through her glasses. She squinted and pulled them off her face. "Of course, come on in," she said and pointed to the chair on the other side of her desk. "Want some coffee?" She was already turning around and pouring him a cup from the carafe that sat behind her.

"Thanks," he said and reached for the large paper cup. He opened his mouth to ask for a packet of sugar, but she was already grabbing it.

"And a splash of cream, right?" She picked up the insulated container and put that in front of him as well.

He looked up from pouring in his packet of sugar, trying to hide his surprise. "Uh, yes, that's right."

She dipped her head and cleared her throat, pointing to his coffee cup. "Freeze alert. I saw how you liked your coffee."

"I did consume a lot those nights—well, early mornings," he chuckled.

She hummed in agreement and her eyes went to the folder Cal had set on the desk. "This the info for the biodynamic certification?"

"Oh, yes." He pulled the folder to him and opened it, giving her the first part. He waited as she read through it, trying not to watch her for any length of time. She'd slipped back on her reading glasses, and the hair that had been tucked behind her ear kept falling forward into her face. He held in a smile as she repeatedly brought her hand up, quick with impatience, and tucked it back.

As she turned the second page, she glanced up at him, and Cal suddenly realized he'd been staring. It was obvious she had a question on her tongue, but her expression froze, and Cal felt his cheeks grow hot. "Um, do we need a big variety of livestock before starting the process? Or can we just have goats?"

He shuffled the remaining papers in his folder as if searching for the answer. He already knew it; he needed a second to recover. "We can stick with goats. They'll give us sufficient material for composting and of course help with weed abatement. We can even get into the goat cheese business down the line."

She looked back down at the paper and Cal sat back in his seat, his eyes fixed on a small wooden box Mia had next to her computer monitor. He wondered what was in it, guessing it must be important to her.

"One business at a time, Cal." Mia's tone was light, and the corner of her lips quirked up before she got an introspective look on her face. "What do you think about chickens, though?"

They spent the next half an hour discussing logistics and making an appointment to go look at goats—and chickens—from a nearby farm.

"I'll get Freddie to help me with building the chicken coop and goat enclosure," Cal said as he stood to leave.

"I can help too. I'd love to learn how to be more handy."

"Of course. That would be great." Cal smiled.

Mia stood and walked Cal to the door. "Okay, good. Start tomorrow?"

"Sure. I'll run into town with Freddie and get what we need, and we can spend the afternoon building."

"Okay. See you tomorrow, Cal."

"See you tomorrow."

Cal bounded down the stairs, going over the day's tasks in an attempt to stave off the excitement he felt at spending more time with Mia. She was his boss, a widow, and he had absolutely no business thinking of her as anyone else.

MIA FURROWED HER BROW IN CONCENTRATION AS SHE measured the piece of wood, marked it, and then used a triangle to draw the line. "Now we take it to the saw and line up the blade with the line." She picked up the two-by-four and set it down under the blade like she'd seen him do. "Okay, bring the blade down, but don't press the button. We need to make sure it's placed correctly." She did as she was told, being very careful not to put her fingers anywhere near the blade or the button.

She brought it down so that the blade touched the line and looked at Cal. "Like this, right?"

"Yep. Now bring it back up, press the button and bring it down slowly and then back up slowly."

She pushed her safety glasses further up her nose and checked her fingers once again and then grabbed the handle, pressed the button, and brought the saw down smoothly and then back up.

"Perfect," Cal said with an approving smile. "You've got this down. You know how to use a screw gun, how to check for level, and how to measure and cut wood. The basics of building. Now, are you ready to put it all together?"

"Yep," she said, looking at all the wood they'd cut, the box of screws, and the rolls of chicken wire. It seemed daunting. When there was no response from Cal, she turned to him, catching his amused smile. "What?" Her tone was indignant, but her tiny smile took any sting out of it.

"You look skeptical."

Mia shrugged. "You said you've built a few of these over the years. I trust that you know what you're doing."

He stepped closer and folded his arms over his chest. "I appreciate the vote of confidence." His smirk was playful, and Mia felt herself caught up for a moment.

"I think you've earned it... so far."

His eyes widened a bit at the last part of her sentence, and she gave him her own smirk. He was about to respond when Samuel came through the gate and surveyed all the building material. "What are you guys building?"

"Chicken coop," Mia answered and then walked over to the board she'd just cut and threw the part they needed into the pile.

"Need help?"

Cal looked at Mia and read the slight widening of her eyes. "No, we got it, thanks."

"You sure? I'm sure Mia has better things—"

"I volunteered to help. I wanted to learn some new skills," Mia interrupted him as she picked up the screw gun. Her tone was somewhat terse, but once again, Cal sensed her unease.

"She's a quick study. We'll have this coop done in no time. Thanks for the offer, though." Cal's tone was cordial but dismissing, and luckily Samuel got the hint.

"Okay, well, I'll leave you to it then," Samuel said slowly. He lingered for another few seconds before turning back the way he came.

Cal watched Mia's eyes as they followed Samuel out of the gate until he was out of sight. She let out a sigh and looked at Cal. "I... know he's a good worker, and he does his job well, but sometimes..." Cal waited to see if Mia would continue, but she abandoned whatever she was going to say and pointed at the stack of two-by-fours with a raised eyebrow. "We gonna build this coop, or what?"

"Sure. Let's do it." Cal smiled as he picked up two pieces of wood and asked Mia to grab the box of screws.

It took a couple of hours, but right before sunset, they had a sturdy-looking chicken coop.

"Wow, that was pretty fun," Mia said as she put her hands on her hips and nodded. She looked at Cal and smiled. "We work well together."

"Teamwork makes the dream work," he said as he raised a hand for a high five which she eagerly gave. "Want to help me with the goat enclosure tomorrow?"

Mia felt her lips curve into a big smile. "Absolutely."

Cal checked the hitch one more time before getting into his truck. He and Mia were headed to pick up the goats and chickens in a nearby town that morning and they had borrowed a livestock trailer from the farm across the road from the winery. He was opening the driver door when he heard someone approaching.

"You gonna be gone all day?"

He turned to see Samuel standing there, hands on his hips.

"Most of it. Freddie's got the task list." Cal got into his truck, rolling his eyes as he heard Samuel's boot heels strike the ground with more force necessary as he stalked away.

"Let's go see a man about some goats," Cal said after he slid into his seat and started the engine.

"And chickens," Mia added as she put on her seatbelt, seemingly unaware of the brief conversation between Cal and Samuel. "I'm excited for fresh eggs."

Cal nodded in agreement. "Hey, have you gotten anywhere with the letters I found?" he asked.

Mia smiled excitedly. "A little bit. They were all written by someone named Anne Harris to Patty Giambi, the youngest daughter of the original owners. At first, I thought they were childhood pals, but..." When she trailed off, Cal looked at her curiously. "I think, well, it was quite obvious that they must have been lovers. But apparently, Patty never wrote back. The first half dozen letters were all about Anne's training as a test pilot and the women she met on base. It was quite fascinating, actually. I should probably copy them for an archive."

"She was a test pilot?" Cal asked, intrigued.

"Yeah, from what I could gather, she flew her father's crop duster when he was too drunk to do it himself. She was recruited by the Air Force. Part of the WASP."

"That is fascinating," Cal said.

Mia nodded and then sighed. "After those letters it was

obvious Patty wasn't writing back. Anne seemed pretty distraught, wondering if she was okay then speculating that she'd found a beau, or boyfriend, I guess. The last one broke my heart. Anne seemed devastated she hadn't written back. It was dated July 1943. I wonder why she never wrote back?"

Cal thought about how he found the letters. How they didn't look like they'd even been opened. "I wonder if Patty never got them?"

Mia turned in her seat, eyes wide. "Like someone hid them from her? And then put them up in the attic all those years ago?"

Cal shrugged. "It's certainly a possibility."

Mia sat back with a grunt of surprise. "This definitely gives me another angle to research. How sad if it's true, though, huh?"

Cal hummed in agreement. "It was such a different time back then. Anne was pretty brave to write those letters."

"Yes, she was," Mia said quietly as she sat back a bit deeper in her seat and stared out the windshield. "What she wrote... she seemed to really be in love with Patty." Her voice was thick with emotion and Cal didn't know what to say. Was Mia thinking about her husband? Was she moved or disturbed by romantic love between two women?

There were a few moments of silence between them before Mia spoke again. "This biodynamic certification—it is worth it, right? It's a good investment of money?"

There was an undercurrent of worry in her tone and Cal rushed to reassure her. "Yes, especially here on the central coast. It will take a little while to get set up and the benefits will take some time to come through—both financially and ecologically—but this type of land care, it is the future. Plus, you'll have the immediate added revenue stream of renting out the goats."

"Okay. I just... want to make sure this plan is sound."

The tone of her voice made him turn and look at her. Her eyes were still looking straight ahead, but he could see the bunching of muscles in her jaw.

"You all right, Mia?"

She turned to look at him but didn't speak for a few seconds. His eyes went back to the road for an instant, then he looked back at her with concern.

"The winery is all I have, Cal. My husband, Tom, made a couple of bad investments. I had no idea until after his death. Everything I have is wrapped up in it. Everything."

Cal's eyes returned to the road out of necessity, and he took in a slow breath and let it out. He'd taken the job to prove himself primarily, but ever since Mia had joined him out in the rows and asked him to teach her about pruning, he'd been invested in her success just as much. He'd seen something in her that day and nearly every day after—a love for the land, an appreciation for everything on it. He wanted the winery to succeed not only for him professionally, but because Mia owned it.

It was why he proposed the idea of biodynamic farming. He had a feeling she'd see the value in it, both for the land and financially. He was not disappointed.

Cal knew she wasn't looking for platitudes about what she'd just said. So, he didn't offer any. He nodded at her solemnly, right before his map app instructed him to turn right and then they'd be at their destination. "You ready to learn the art of goat wrangling?" Cal had his hand on the door handle as he grinned over at Mia.

"Ready as I'll ever be."

7

Cal closed the gate and let out a heaving sigh as he rested his forearms on top of it. "I kinda wish we would have recorded that. I'm pretty sure we would have gone viral."

Mia blew out a breath that made strands of hair that had slipped out of her ponytail and into her face flutter about comically. "That was... something. I'm glad one of us knew what we were doing." She bent down to wipe at the knees of her jeans, but it was a lost cause. They were stained with mud and had bits of straw embedded in the fabric.

"I'm not too sure it showed today." Cal laughed recalling the shitshow that was getting all the goats out of the trailer and forgetting they get very skittish in open spaces. Loading them directly into the enclosure would have been best, but he'd been distracted by Mia's excitement. She was already naming them as they drove back to the vineyard.

Because of his mistake, they'd spent two hours trying to round the goats up from the paddock. Cal and Mia had spent equal time laughing and cursing as the goats ran around bleating and nipping at them. Both had ended up on the ground more than once trying to catch the wily animals.

"How do you feel about ordering pizza?" Mia said as she straightened up, pulled her hair tie out, and tried to smooth her hair back into some semblance of order.

"I feel great about ordering pizza. I think I really need to shower first, if that's okay?" Cal could smell himself a good hour ago.

"Yeah, I do too. I'll meet you up at the house in thirty minutes?"

"Sounds good," Cal said, and with a quick wave he jogged over to his set of stairs and took them two at a time. As he let himself into his apartment and headed to the shower, he thought about how much he'd enjoyed the day spent with Mia.

When he was hired, he hadn't anticipated spending much time with the winery owner. But Mia had been a lot more hands on than Jose had described. Was she just making sure Cal was doing a good job?

He thought about their conversation in the truck on the way to the farm when she'd told him how her late husband had left her in debt with her only asset being the winery.

She also said that she trusted Cal. Trusted him to do what needed to be done to make the winery profitable. It was a huge responsibility, but one he was more than willing to take on. He was also excited to turn the winery into a biodynamic farm. The benefits would be tremendous, as would the potential for other revenue streams should Mia want to pursue them.

Dressed in a clean pair of jeans and a navy long-sleeve Henley, he shoved his feet back into his boots right by the front door and grabbed his keys.

He pulled into Mia's driveway the same time the pizza

delivery driver arrived. He paid the guy and took the pizza and then knocked on Mia's door.

"Oh, hey, good timing," Mia said with a surprised smile as she opened the door to let Cal in. She took the pizza and gestured for him to follow her. Her hair was still wet from the shower and hung in loose ringlets about halfway down her back. As Cal trailed after her, he took in the fresh clean scent of citrus she left in her wake.

"You've never been inside the house, have you?" Mia asked, her voice lilting up in realization.

"Nope," Cal said as he took the opportunity to look around. His eyes were automatically drawn to the ceiling, and he admired the large rough-hewn exposed beams. The walls were a dark cream color with heavily textured stucco and the doors and baseboards were trimmed out with wide, dark-stained wood. "It's gorgeous."

"Thank you, it really came out beautifully. When we bought the place, it needed some remodeling, but I wanted to keep the integrity of the style. I do love how it turned out." Mia smiled proudly as she rounded a corner and then they were in the spacious kitchen with the same dark stain for the cabinets with light quartz countertops.

"Want a beer?" Mia asked as she set the pizza box down on the large island.

"Water would be great. Can I get us some plates?" Cal asked.

"First cabinet to the left of the sink." Mia instructed as she grabbed a couple of glasses from another cabinet and filled them with water from the fridge.

They met at the island and Mia opened the pizza box. She paused and looked at Cal with an apologetic smile. "I didn't know what kind you liked, so I got a little bit of everything."

Cal waved her off. "My mom used to call me a human garbage can. I eat everything."

Mia laughed and slid the box toward Cal. "Well, that's good to know."

He took two slices and slid it back. "I'm pretty easy." He immediately felt his cheeks tingle and took a big bite to hide his mild discomfort at the double entendre. He didn't dare look up at Mia.

"Are you close with her?" Mia asked after an awkward but brief silence. Cal was grateful for the question even if it was a hard one to answer.

"I was. She was the best. She died five years ago of a brain aneurysm."

"Oh, Cal. I'm so sorry... It's so hard... when it's sudden like that."

Cal nodded as he swallowed his bite of pizza with effort. His father rarely wanted to talk about losing his mom. He and his sister were left to deal with her death mostly on their own. "It is hard. There were so many things I wanted to say to her, you know? At the very least, tell her how much I loved her and appreciated her..." He blinked back tears as he picked up his glass of water.

"I'm sorry... I shouldn't have..." Mia's words came out in a rush as she shook her head, eyes dropping down to her plate.

"No, it's okay. I don't mind." Cal watched her, waiting for her to look back up at him. When she did, the corner of Cal's lips lifted into a half-smile. "I don't think you're ever prepared to lose someone, whether it's sudden or not."

"Yeah..." Mia's voice was soft, introspective and Cal focused on his pizza, feeling like an intruder as her eyes went to the kitchen window, mind caught up in a memory. "My mom got sick when I was young. She had breast cancer, a real aggressive type that was caught late. She fought as long as she could, but she died six months after her diagnosis."

"How old were you?" Cal asked as a knot formed in his stomach.

"I was thirteen."

Cal sighed. "That's so rough, Mia. I'm so sorry."

Her smile was pained but appreciative. "I could tell how much it was hurting her, leaving me. She signed up for every clinical trial she was able to, just to give us a few weeks, a few days. Her body gave out way before her will did." Cal didn't know what else to say. Every word in the English language felt insufficient.

"Can you tell me about her?"

Mia pushed her plate to the side and put her elbows on the counter. Her eyes shone with unshed tears but the wrinkles in the corners of her eyes creased deeply as she smiled. "She was a badass." Mia laughed. "She had me fairly young. My father wasn't involved at all. She put herself through school, working two jobs when I was younger to become a nurse."

"Was it only you and her then?" Cal asked.

"Yep. I remember her bringing me to one of her jobs at a coffee shop. The manager told her she couldn't, but she threatened to quit on the spot and tell customers there were rats in the kitchen. She then plunked me down at the corner of the counter with a coloring book, a box of borrowed crayons, and a wink. I loved being around her."

"She does sound like a badass." Cal chuckled.

"How about your mom?"

"She was very sweet. Kind of old fashioned. She loved to cook. I'd help her with her vegetable garden she had out back. She grew all kinds of herbs and would tell me what they were used in. She tried to get me to learn, but all I wanted to do was be outside catching frogs and lighting stuff on fire."

He couldn't explain that when he lived as a girl, his mom thought he should learn how to cook because he'd be marrying a man and would need to know how. When he'd come out as a lesbian, she still insisted it important he learn to cook for himself. Then, when he came out to her as trans, it took a couple of months for her to come around, but she had, and had been his biggest supporter up until the day she died. And she never gave up trying to teach him to cook. How he'd wished he could have gone back in time and learned because that meant he would have spent more time with her.

"I hope you've grown out of the fire-starting." Mia teased, bringing him out of his thoughts.

"Mostly. There will be instances we'll need to do controlled burns, though." He waved his finger in the air. "I do live for those days."

She shook her head and rolled her eyes. "I had no idea I hired a pyromaniac."

Cal gave her an exaggerated sorry-about-it shrug.

"Guess I'm gonna have to fire you."

Cal groaned at the bad pun and then laughed with surprise when Mia balled up her napkin and threw it at him.

"I thought it was pretty funny."

Cal dug the napkin out of the puddle of grease it was rapidly absorbing on his uneaten slice and playfully glared at her. "Eh, it kind of flamed out, to be honest."

Mia balled up another napkin but then let it drop from her fingers as they both started laughing in earnest.

8

Mia poured herself another half-glass of wine and took a sip. After she'd come back from her office and made herself a quick pasta dinner, she had opened up her laptop to do a little more research on the letters Cal found.

She'd stumbled upon a website dedicated to the history of wineries on the central coast and had found a whole page on the Giambi Winery. "Hmm." Mia grunted as one caught her eye—a couple standing in front of the then-fairly new barn. She smiled wistfully at just how pristine and bright it had been before concentrating on the people. There was a woman, head turned toward a man, and though Mia only saw her profile, her luminous smile was evident. She was leaning into the man, and he had his arm around her, facing the camera with a broad grin. The caption read *Adam and Patty Howe 1952*.

Mia leaned in closer, studying the man. His thick dark hair was in stark contrast to his clear, incandescent eyes. Even though the photo was black and white Mia could easily picture his bright blue eyes. His clean-shaven, heart-shaped jaw looked like it was bisected by a large scar that started at the middle of his cheek. He was also more slight and about an inch shorter than Patty was.

"Howe..." Mia murmured as she opened another tab on her browser and typed in the name along with Giambi Winery. A digital copy of an old newspaper article from 1976 popped up and she leaned in to read it.

Adam Howe, Vice President of Operations for the Giambi Winery passed away on the property July 8th, 1976. He was born in Kansas City, Kansas May 14, 1921 to Reginald and Margaret Howe.

He made his way to California after World War II ended and met Patricia Giambi while working as a day laborer for her father Paolo Giambi. Many say it was love at first sight. They were married on August 21, 1946.

Adam was a loyal husband and doting father and spent years earning his way up to the position he held at Giambi Winery until his death. He worked tirelessly to make the Giambi Winery one of the premiere purveyors of syrah in the region. He will be missed for his work ethic and warm and inviting personality.

He is survived by his loving wife, Patricia and their two adopted children, Kyle and Margaret. Services will be held at the estate on July 15 at 2 p.m. Open to the public.

"How did you die, Adam?" she asked aloud as she started a new search. It took some digging, but she found an old newspaper article about a wildfire that had destroyed a couple of wineries and damaged about half a dozen. The article said that Adam and another worker had perished while trying to fight the fire as it encroached onto the vineyard.

She pushed away from the table as her mind went to the day Tom died. She closed her eyes and took a breath as all the emotions of that day came up in quick succession. They were muted with the passage of time, but always there, right under the surface. The confusion, the shock, the helplessness, and finally the disbelief quickly followed by abject sorrow. Her world had tilted on its axis in a matter of minutes, and she'd been fighting to gain her balance ever since.

"Okay... okay," she said slowly as she opened her eyes and took a couple more long, deep breaths. She pulled herself back to her desk and her computer and went back to the photo. She smiled unconsciously as she took in the details of the barn, just a few years old at the time.

She opened another tab on her browser and typed 'Anne Harris test pilot World War II' into the search bar. "Wow, there are a lot of Anne Harrises in the world," Mia mumbled as she scrolled through the results. Finally, on the second page she found an article featuring her on a website dedicated to the history of the WASP.

Anne Marie Harris joined the WASPs when she was twenty-two-years old. She was born and raised in Paso Robles, California and got her start as a pilot at a young age flying crop dusters for her father's business. She quickly made a name for herself as one of the best test pilots in her class, earning several commendations. Her flight instructor, Lieutenant Arthur Dimwittle had this to say about her: *'That Anne, she's a helluva gal who could make any bird she was flyin' sing!'*

On July 23rd, 1943, while transporting a P-51 Mustang from California to Delaware, she disappeared, presumed to have crashed somewhere in the Rocky Mountains. The remains of the wreckage and her body have still yet to be found.

She hadn't realized she was crying until she felt a warm,

wet tear track down her cheek. She wiped it away with the back of her hand. Her heart hurt for the young woman. Had she and Patty ever reconnected? Or were those the last words Anne wrote to her in that letter?

There was a photo of Anne that went with the article and Mia leaned forward to look at the slightly grainy photo of a slight woman with wavy hair and a wide smile standing next to a C-19, resplendent in her uniform and bomber jacket. Even with the poor quality, the lightness of her eyes stood out. She cocked her head as she clicked back the photo of Patty and Adam. She opened another window and put the photos side by side. "Wow," she whispered. The resemblance was uncanny. She picked up her wine glass and sat back, taking another sip as she continued to stare at the two photos.

Were they siblings? Had Adam started courting Patty after Anne went missing? Or before? Was there even something going on between Anne and Patty, or was it all in Anne's head? Her search for answers had only unearthed more questions. *Cal would be interested in this development.* She looked up at the clock at the top right corner of her screen and her eyes widened. Not only was it too late to text Cal, but it was also way past her bedtime.

She bookmarked the pages and closed her laptop then gathered her empty glass and dishes, left forgotten on the kitchen table. She took them to the sink, absently rinsing them as she thought about the information she'd found. There must be a heck of a story behind those letters and Mia was as excited to share this all with Cal as she was to figure out the mystery.

As she climbed the stairs to her bedroom, she thought about Cal. How she'd been skeptical at first that he could do the job. But she'd trusted Jose's judgment and so far, he's been right. There was something about him that put Mia at ease.

She thought about her conversation with Lloyd. She missed her friend a lot and was looking forward to him visiting. Outside of Tom, he knew her best. She wondered what he would think of Cal. She paused on the stairs when it hit her just how much she hoped Lloyd liked him.

CAL LOOKED OUT OVER THE SECTION OF LAND AS HE WALKED along the western perimeter of the grapevine rows. "This really is the only spot we can do it, Jefe," Freddie said.

"You're right." Cal shaded his eyes as he focused on the large oak tree at the south end. It threw off a lot of shade and it would be tricky to get anything to grow in it's shadow.

Freddie came up to stand next to him. "It's a good tree. Could make lots of furniture."

Cal hated cutting down trees, but sometimes it was a necessary evil in farming. "I'll talk to Mrs. Torwood about it."

"You can ask her right now." Freddie grinned as he waved to Mia who was riding Lucas along the rows toward them. He turned back to Cal. "I'm going to head back. Let me know what she says."

"Will do." Cal nodded. He watched Mia come up next to his truck, parked about fifty yards away. She dismounted and loosely tied Lucas' reigns to his bumper. A wide smile crept across Cal's lips, but he tempered it by the time Mia was approaching him.

"I was out for a ride before work and thought I'd stop and see what you guys were up to," Mia said as she picked her way through the rough, rock-strewn earth before coming to a stop right in front of Cal. "So, this is where you think you might plant the companion crops?"

"Yes, except that oak throws off a huge amount of shade. I was wondering if we might be able to cut it down." Mia stepped past him and headed toward the big tree. He followed behind her.

When she reached it, she lifted a hand and ran it down the trunk slowly, looking up at it. "Seems a shame to cut it down."

"I'm really on the fence about it too," he said as he walked around the tree, looking up into its branch system. *Maybe...*

"Hey, Cal, come here, please." Mia called to him. He walked over to her, standing closely behind and to the side of her as she pointed up at something on the tree. "Do you see that?" Cal stepped a little closer so he could follow her sight line.

He was momentarily distracted as he took in a breath and caught a very pleasant scent of linen and citrus. He couldn't tell if it was her perfume or shampoo, but he really liked it. "See it? About eight feet up?" Cal refocused, squinting as he searched. His eyes widened as he found it—a crudely cut heart with the initials A+P in the middle. There was something else, smaller, carved below the initials.

They both looked at each other, eyes holding for a long second. A warmth caught in his chest as they exchanged excited smiles. He liked having this mystery connect them. "I'm going to go get the truck, get a better look."

"Better untie Lucas from your bumper then." She laughed.

"Right," he said with a chuckle.

Cal pulled up as close to the tree as he could and climbed into the bed. He rose up on the toes of his boots and leaned out, stretching his hand out to brace himself against the tree. "It's a date. Four…" He leaned forward, straining to read the rest. "Twelve… Forty."

"April 12th, 1940?" Mia speculated.

"That's what it looks like, unless it's a combination code," Cal shrugged with a crooked grin.

Mia's brow furrowed as she muttered, "The newspaper obituary said Patty and Adam didn't meet until after World War Two…"

"Adam?" Cal asked in confusion.

"Oh, right, I didn't get a chance to tell you yet. I was doing some more digging and found out that Patty married a man named Adam, but his obituary said they didn't meet until after the war."

The thought of Patty moving on and marrying someone else made Cal inexplicably sad. He gave the carving one more look before he jumped out of the bed of his truck. "Huh… Well, maybe it *is* Anne and Patty?"

Mia shrugged, nodding as she put her hands on her hips. "Well, one thing is for sure. We can't cut this tree down now."

Cal ran his hand over his beard and looked up again. "Yeah, you're right. I can trim it down though, let some light through. Would that be okay?"

Mia nodded slowly. "I think so."

"Okay. I'm going to call Freddie down. Light's good to get started. I can finish up tomorrow and start tilling the field. Gotta get everything into the ground as soon as we can."

MIA WATCHED CAL SCALE THE TALL LADDER. SHE DID HAVE some work to get back to, but once Freddie had come down with the tools to trim the tree, Mia felt the need to stay and watch.

"You worried I'm going to mess the tree up or you looking to catch me if I fall?" Cal called down to Mia as he stepped off the ladder and onto a thick branch.

She wasn't fond of heights, and her stomach tightened as she watched him balance with one hand on an upper branch while the other held a saw. "Neither, to be honest," she said, loud enough for him to hear. He looked down at her with a smirk. "Just... be careful please. Can't have you out of commission."

"No worries. I've trimmed plenty of trees and a few even bigger than this one. Watch out for falling branches, though." His eyes were already tracking a medium-sized branch growing off the big one he was standing on. He knelt down, sawed three-quarters of the way through and then stood clear of it when it gave way and fell to the ground.

Mia watched as he maneuvered his way around, taking out branch after branch in an evenly distributed pattern. He did move pretty well from branch to branch, and Mia's concern leveled out the longer she watched him.

"All right, Freddie, I'm moving up to remove the ones near the top. Throw up the rope." Mia watched with interest as Freddie tossed a heavy rope up to Cal who deftly caught it with one hand. He dropped down, straddling the branch he had been standing on, tied the saw to the rope and lowered it down on the other side of the branch. Freddie untied it and then tied the larger one on. He pulled on the slack side of the rope until it reached Cal who took the saw and tied the rope to the branch.

Cal had been at it for a good two hours and the sun was dipping lower and lower. He stopped more often to wipe the sweat from his brow as Freddie pointed to which branches should be left and which could be cut. As if reading Mia's mind, Cal looked down. "Almost done for the day. I'm gonna get this last one since I'm up here."

"Okay," Mia said, relieved. He was at least twenty feet off the ground and balancing on smaller branches. She held her breath as he balanced the saw against the trunk of the tree and the branch above him. In an impressive show of upper body strength, he pulled himself up and onto the branch, electing to straddle it instead of stand on it.

He scooted out slowly, saw under his arm, until he got to the branch Freddie had pointed out. As he was reaching up to it, a loud crack reverberated through the warm, still air.

"Cal?" Mia shouted worriedly.

"Jefe..." Freddie called up, his tone carrying the same concern.

"I'm gonna drop the saw down and back up." Mia could hear the tremor in Cal's voice as he carelessly dropped the saw and gripped the branch he was straddling with both hands. He got about a foot before another, louder crack spiked through the silence. "Aw, fuck." Cal managed before the branch gave way.

Mia watched in horror as Cal was pitched forward and off the branch completely. He was heading toward the ground headfirst and all Mia could do was stand, frozen to her spot, heart in her throat. "Jefe!" Freddie cried as he stepped closer to the tree as if he were going to catch Cal.

Miraculously, Cal was able to twist his body enough so that his shoulder connected with one of the branches about halfway down and he managed to grab hold of one of the lower branches for a second, slowing his ascent. He still landed on the ground in a dull thud, but on his side, not his head or neck.

Mia's feet were moving before she even registered it and

she slid to her knees about a foot from Cal's prone body. "Cal?" she cried, afraid to even touch him for fear of injuring him further. "Cal?" She tried again, this time gingerly touching his back.

"Mr. Sanders?" Freddie called loudly as he bent over him. Freddie and Mia looked at each other, faces both stricken with panic until a rasping groan brought their eyes down to Cal.

"Did that seriously just fucking happen?" He moaned as he shifted to his back. Mia reached out as if to stop him but retracted her hands when she saw he seemed mostly okay.

"It sure did, Jefe. Are you okay?" Relief and amusement were evident in Freddie's voice and Mia took that as a positive sign. She let out a breath, feeling the bands of worry loosen around her heart.

"Give me a minute," Cal grimaced as he lifted one leg and then the other. He opened his eyes and then worked his jaw a few times before turning his head slowly from side to side.

"What is your full name?" Mia asked. She'd seen people do that on television when someone fell and hit their head.

"Cal James Sanders."

"What day is it?" Mia continued.

"Friday, April twenty-third."

Mia held up her hand. "How many fingers am I holding up?"

Cal's slight grimace turned into a crooked grin as he squinted his eyes. "Three. Am I gonna live, doc?"

Mia sat back on her heels, not amused at Cal's casual tone. "That scared the shit out of me—us," Mia stammered, eyes going to Freddie who nodded vigorously.

Cal's grin faded, and he made a move to sit up, but when he put weight on his left arm, he yelped and pulled it into his chest. "I'm sorry about that. Damn branch. Also, I think I might have broken my arm."

Mia looked down at the arm in question and then back up into Cal's glassy eyes. "I'll drive you to the ER."

Cal's eyes fell open wide. "No! That's okay." He scrambled onto his right, using that arm to push himself all the way up. When he stood, he swayed.

"Cal..." Mia said, her tone a mix of sympathy and reprimand.

"Mrs. Torwood's right. I'll stay and clean up. You get checked out, Jefe." Freddie offered. Cal gave him a stern look.

"No one likes hospitals, Cal, but you have to have that arm x-rayed." Mia reasoned as she pointed to the arm he was cradling.

"I know. I will. I can get myself there," Cal said as he started off toward his truck. Mia followed him.

"You're in no condition to drive, Cal," Mia said as she came up next to him.

"It's just my arm. I'll be okay to drive," he said, not breaking stride as he yanked the truck door open with his good hand but still winced. It didn't seem like Cal to be so stubborn, and Mia wondered if he hit his head harder than what she'd witnessed.

"Don't be ridiculous. I can take you."

"You have Lucas," Cal said as he pointed to the horse, grazing on the wildflowers about twenty feet from the truck.

Mia called back to Freddie. "Freddie! Can you take Lucas back to the barn?"

"Of course, Mrs. Torwood! No worry!"

Mia focused on Cal, eyebrow raised. Cal's shoulders slumped in resignation. He looked truly perturbed as he sighed heavily and walked around to the passenger side of the truck and slid in, albeit gingerly.

"You don't seem like the pigheaded type," Mia said after the silence stretched on for an uncomfortable amount of time. Cal hadn't said a word since they'd turned from the property drive onto the road that would take them to the hospital about twenty-five minutes away. "Do you hate hospitals that much?"

She glanced at him as his eyes left the passenger side window to look directly out the windshield. "I haven't had the best experiences with them."

"Well, yeah, no one really does," Mia said, remembering sitting by her mother's bedside, watching her slowly deteriorate.

"It's not—" Cal started but then cut himself off. "Can you drop me off at the door? I've got my insurance card and stuff in my wallet."

There was something in Cal's tone that made Mia turn to look at him. His eyes were wide, glistening, but she didn't think it was from pain. Fear?

When she opened her mouth to argue, he pinned her with a pleading look. "Please. I need to go in by myself."

Mia turned her eyes back to the road. "Okay, Cal. I'll drop you off. I'll go run some errands and you call me as soon as you're done." She knew it sounded like an order, but she wanted it to be clear she wasn't just going to drop him off and leave him.

"I will. Thanks for the ride," he said as they pulled up to the hospital ER department.

"Well, it's your truck," Mia said with a wan smile.

"True." He nodded as he opened the door and got out carefully. He faced her, jaw set and eyes rueful. "I hope it doesn't take too long... you can—"

Mia cut him off. "I'll be here when you're done."

He regarded her for a moment before he nodded once. "Okay. Thanks again." He closed the door and stepped back, actually waiting for her to drive off. She waved and pulled away from the curb.

Why was he so dead set on her not going in with him? It seemed kind of out of character for him to be so obstinate, but he obviously had a reason and felt strongly about it.

She pulled into a home improvement store parking lot a mile away and called Freddie to make sure Lucas was put away okay, then took a look at the running list she had of items the ranch house always seemed to need. She knew it was going to be a good few hours before Cal would be ready to go home.

9

"Make sure to follow up with your primary doctor in a week, Mr. Sanders," Dr. Linn said as she handed him a prescription for pain meds. "And try to stay out of trees." She delivered the last sentence with a crooked grin and Cal ducked his head.

"I'll try. Thanks, doctor," he said as he slipped off the table. He inspected the black fiberglass cast and sighed. It would hinder a lot of the work he had to get done in the next couple of weeks. He'd need to do some delegating.

He made his way out of the maze of corridors and checked out at the reception desk. Once outside, he took out his phone and called Mia. "Hey Mia, if you're still around, I'm all done."

"Great timing. I was about to grab something to eat at a burger place. I'll get it to go. What would you like?"

Cal nearly salivated at the thought of food. He was starving. "That would be awesome, thank you. I'll take a cheeseburger, everything on it, fries and a root beer, please."

"You got it. Be there in about fifteen minutes."

"Sounds good. I'll hang out. Thanks again. For everything. I owe you." Cal hated putting people out. It made him feel uncomfortable. But he could admit to himself he was glad it was Mia who had driven him to the hospital, even if he had been terrified of her going in with him.

"You don't owe me anything, Cal. I'll be there in a bit." She ended the call and Cal slipped the phone back in his pocket. He took a seat on the bench near the emergency drop off area and took in a deep breath and let it out slow.

Ever since transitioning, encounters with medical personnel had been anxiety-inducing experiences. He never knew how he'd be treated and always had to mentally prepare to be misunderstood, misgendered, or outright humiliated.

It was easier now that he was fully transitioned and all his documentation reflected that, but it still came up and he'd have to disclose himself. When he was undressing in the curtained-off bay, he made sure to keep his back to where the curtain opened into the larger area. The hair on his chest mostly hid the scars, but they were still visible if one looked closely enough.

Since he was in for a broken arm—clean break of the ulna midway between his elbow and wrist—there was no reason for any type of invasive treatment. To all concerned, he was just Cal Sanders, a man who fell out of a tree and broke his arm.

He couldn't help the guilt that accompanied these types of situations, though. He knew transgender visibility was the key to battling ignorance and hatred. But he wanted a simple life. One that was his alone that he could live happily on his own terms. There was a comfort, a safety in passing; he was loath to give that up.

He'd done his time in his old life in the central valley. He'd endured homophobic slurs when he identified as a butch lesbian. He'd had his life threatened by one of his father's closest business associates because he'd given his daughter a ride home when her car broke down. He'd had his heart broken when he put himself out there as a newly out trans man, thinking he was finally ready to start dating.

All he wanted was to be able to grow amazing wine grapes and make a name for himself as a top-tier vintner. Keeping his head down and doing the best job he could with Torwood Winery was the best way to someday own his own winery, using *his* methods and experience.

The one thing he hadn't counted on though—and in fact was studiously trying to ignore—was how he was starting to feel about the owner of Torwood Winery. The more he got to know her, the more he could feel himself being drawn to her.

He looked up as he heard the familiar rumbling of his diesel engine. He stood and waved his casted arm as he walked to the curb. "Hey, looks like you really did break it, huh?" Mia said as she picked up the bag of food from the passenger seat so he could slide in.

Cal used his good arm to pull himself up into the cab and once he was settled with his seatbelt on, he held out his hand to hold the bag. "Yep. Clean break. Should be right as rain in about a month or so." Mia eyed him skeptically and he let out a mildly indignant breath. "I'm telling you the truth. I have a follow-up with a regular doctor in a week. I guess I need to find one now."

Mia looked down at his cast and then back up to his eyes. "Okay. I believe you. I can call my primary doctor. She's great and I know she'll be able to get you in."

Cal gave her a tight nod. He knew as soon as he said he needed to find a doctor, Mia would offer up someone she knew. He mentally shook off the paranoia though.

Whomever he saw wouldn't go sharing his private medical information with Mia. "Sounds good. Want to park so we can eat? Or are you in a hurry to get back?" Cal asked, holding up the bag.

Mia considered the question for a second. "No big hurry. Safer to park and eat, anyway." She found a spot down one of the back rows and pulled into it with relative ease. Considering Cal's truck was a pretty good size, he was impressed. He knew she drove a medium-sized SUV when she wasn't getting around on her golf cart.

Cal handed Mia her burger and upon seeing she hadn't ordered any fries, ripped the top off the bag, poured his fries in and set it on the console. "Help yourself to the fries. There's plenty."

Mia looked at him right before taking a bite of her burger. There was a hint of a smile playing at the right corner of her lips. "Thanks."

They ate in companionable silence with Cal doing his level best not to get melted cheese or ketchup into his new cast as he worked the foil wrapper down the burger as he ate.

"Here," Mia said with all the patience of a kindergarten teacher at the end of a long day. There was a ghost of a smile on her face though as Cal handed over his burger. He was way too hungry to refuse the help. She adjusted the wrapper so he could hold it without getting it on his hands and still be able to eat the rest of it without biting into the paper.

"Thanks," he murmured sheepishly as she handed it back to him. Their fingers got tangled up a little on the handoff and a dull heat crept up Cal's neck. "Sorry."

Mia's soft hum was nearly lost in the crinkling of the foil. "No problem. I hated watching you struggle." She laughed lightly as she plucked a fry from the bag and ate it. She then gave Cal a sheepish look. "I didn't want to order fries because they always come in these huge containers, and I can never eat them all."

"Well, for future reference, feel free to order them. I'll finish whatever you don't," Cal said as he dipped his casted hand into the bag and pinched a few fries between his index and middle finger. He stuffed them into his mouth all at once and chewed slowly.

"Noted." Mia took a few more and popped them into her mouth too.

When they were finished eating, Mia collected the trash. "Here, I'll go find a trash can. Pretty sure we don't want to be smelling congealed grease the entire ride home." Before Mia could argue, he got out of the truck and walked back to the ER entrance and threw it away. He started back, but saw that Mia had pulled up by the entrance. "What service." He grinned as he climbed back in.

"Least I could do since you broke your arm in my tree."

Cal shrugged. "Hazard of the job. I've had worse."

"Worse than a broken bone?" Mia turned to look at him before pulling out onto the road.

"Well, I guess the same? It was a summer job. My dad kind of loaned me out to a neighboring farm that had cattle. He wanted me to get some livestock experience." Cal bit his lip, remembering that summer. Remembering the farmer's daughter with whom he'd shared his first kiss. He was still presenting as Callie, a seventeen-year-old butch lesbian.

"Is that why you're so good with goats?" Mia smirked.

Cal's eyes narrowed at her, but he grinned. "Something like that." Mia gestured for him to continue. "Anyway, I was out in the back of the pasture, fixing part of the fence when I hear this loud snort. I turn around and come face to face with a bull from another neighboring ranch. He'd somehow gotten out and was making his way to the heifers. Only problem, I was between him and them."

"Oh no." Mia's voice was low and full of dread.

"Yep. I tried to stand up as slowly as I could, but that was the wrong move. Up and over him I went, landing hard in the dirt. Broke two ribs and put a nice divot under my chin." He brushed where the scar was under his beard. "It's hard to see, but there's a spot where the hair doesn't grow well."

Mia turned her head to look as long as she dared before looking back to the road. "You'll have to show me when we're stopped. That must have been terrifying though, huh? And painful."

Cal shook his head slowly as he recalled that day. "Yeah. it was. I have a healthy fear of bulls now, I can tell you that."

"Well, rest assured, we're only dealing in chickens and goats," Mia laughed.

"I certainly hope so," Cal replied.

"Well, thanks for the ride to the hospital and back. Pretty sure you weren't anticipating getting nothing done for an entire day," Cal said ruefully as he opened the passenger door to get out. Mia watched him as he made sure not to put any weight on his arm. She felt so bad he'd fallen out of the tree.

"It's okay, Cal. Things happen. I'm sorry about your arm. Oh, did you want me to get your prescription filled for you?"

Cal shook his head. "Nah, that's okay. Pain isn't too bad. I'll take some acetaminophen before bed."

"You sure?" Mia asked, brows drawn together in concern.

Cal smiled. "I'm sure. You good to get back up the hill in your golf cart?"

Mia slapped the steering wheel lightly. "Oh, right." She pulled the keys out of the ignition and leaned toward Cal with them. He hesitated to take them.

"You could just drive up to the house in it. I can come get it later."

"No, that's okay. I'll take the golf cart." She leaned a little further and Cal finally took them from her hand. "Take the day off tomorrow, please?"

Cal gave her a half-hearted, dismissive wave. "I'm okay, Mia, really. There's lots I can do with a casted arm. Order people around for sure," he said with a chuckle.

"Oh, that's true. I'm sure Samuel will enjoy that."

They shared a knowing, mildly exasperated look before Cal shrugged. "Well, he can take out his anger on the field; he's gotta help till tomorrow."

Mia climbed out of the truck and came around the back. Cal met her halfway and there was an awkward silence as they stood regarding each other. "Hope you can relax and get some sleep tonight," Mia said. She couldn't understand why she was hesitant to leave. Cal was a grown man.

"Thanks, I'm sure I will. Today was kind of exhausting." He laughed ruefully. "I really appreciate the ride, Mia. Have a good night." Cal smiled and started toward his apartment, leaving her standing there for a moment and wondering what was going on with her.

She walked to her golf cart and got in, but didn't turn it on right away. Instead, she sat there, looking out at the rows of grapevines. The air was cool and fragrant, a sign that spring was in full swing. She sat back in her seat as her mind replayed the eventful day.

She had been so scared when she'd heard the branch crack. While she'd have been just as terrified to watch anyone fall out of a tree twenty-five feet off the ground, the painful catch in her heart those few seconds she was moving to see if he was all right seemed like they took hours. She hadn't been that worried about someone since...

It's because he's an employee, Mia. A very important one. And you get on with him well. She nodded to herself as she leaned down and turned the cart on. *That's all there is to it.*

PART 3: FRUIT SET

10

Mia yawned as she powered up her computer. She hadn't been sleeping well the last couple of weeks and she was beginning to pay for it. She kept dreaming about Cal falling out of the tree, but in those dreams, his injuries were mortal. She took a sip of her coffee as she opened up the accounting program, determined to get done what she needed to.

About half an hour later, there was a knock on her door. "Come in," she called. The door opened, and she was momentarily blinded by the bright sun before it was blocked by the tall, lanky frame of Samuel. She stiffened as he entered her office and closed the door softly behind him.

"Morning, Mia," he said as he stood near the door, his customary floppy straw hat in his hands. He flashed her a small smile but said nothing further as his eyes moved around the area behind her desk, skimming over the pictures sitting behind her then to the large portrait of her and Tom on the wall.

"Morning, Samuel." The use of her first name threw her for a second. She didn't particularly like it coming out of his mouth. She also didn't like the fact he was in her office unannounced. "What can I do for you?"

He looked down at his boots and scratched his head before looking back up at her. He wordlessly gestured to the chair in front of her desk, and she gave him a curt nod. "Well, I wanted to ask... uh, I mean... I wanted to talk to you about Cal and this biodynamic certification. It's a huge undertaking and I don't mind the extra work, but is it really worth it to change our whole system of doing things? I mean, he's only been here a few months and—"

Mia held up a hand. "I trust Cal. Furthermore, he didn't make these decisions on his own. I approved all of them. This is the future of viticulture."

Samuel frowned. "There's a lot of upfront cost to switching over and we don't know how good last year's vintage is gonna sell. Do we have the money for all that?"

It took all of her self-control not to rise up out of her chair and put Samuel in his place. *We? What the hell?* "I appreciate your concern, but I'm very aware of the solvency of *my* winery, Samuel. Was there something else you came in here to ask me? Because if not, I've got a lot of work to do."

His disapproving frown turned into a rueful grimace. "My apologies, Mia. I didn't mean to come across like that. I've been here nearly half my life. This winery... it's like my home. I know change is inevitable. I guess I wasn't ready for it."

Mia sighed softly. His words made sense. His apology sounded sincere. But the uneasy feeling she got every time she was in his presence persisted. As a woman, she'd be remiss to ignore it. But he was a damn good winemaker and with Cal down for at least another two weeks, firing Samuel would create more problems than it would solve.

"Apology accepted. I know change is hard. Now, if there's nothing else, I really do need to get back to work." She tried to keep her polite smile from becoming placative as she regarded him. Her eyes were steady on his and he was the first to look away as he ducked his head slightly, putting his hat back on.

"Thank you for your time, Mia," he said as he stood. He didn't immediately walk to the door though and Mia felt the hair on the back of her neck tingle.

"For what it's worth, I do think you are running the winery as good as any man, including your late husband."

He gave her a very pleased-with-himself grin and walked out of her office, leaving her speechless as she tried to process his words. "What the fuck did that mean?" she muttered to herself as she shook her head in disbelief.

"Mrs. Torwood's gonna be mad at you if she finds out what you're doing."

Cal sighed as he looked over his shoulder at Freddie. "Well, she ain't gonna find out if no one tells her," he said as he turned back around and set the next stake, hammering it into the tilled soil. They'd finally gotten everything planted, but they still had to line the rows with stakes for the beans to grow on.

"Well, you better get that last stake in because she's coming over the hill."

Cal missed the stake head, barely pulling up his hammer strike before smashing into his casted wrist. He growled in frustration. "Dammit, Freddie." He reset his hammer and finally drove the stake the rest of the way in.

"Sorry, Jefe. Thought I'd warn you!"

Freddie's good-natured laugh was lost in the slight breeze and Cal looked up to see a few dark clouds rolling in. "Perfect," he grumbled. He tossed the hammer into the wheelbarrow as Mia appeared on the other side of the hill in her golf cart.

He smiled as he saw her, dressed in her customary faded jeans and button-down flannel shirt. Today was the black and gray one, his favorite. He pulled off his glove, tossing it in the wheelbarrow too and started walking toward her and Freddie.

"Those stakes look good, Freddie. Thanks for getting them in. Looks like rain though, can you get everything gathered up and back to the barn?"

"Sure thing, Jefe," Freddie said with a ridiculous smirk that would surely get him fleeced at any poker game.

Cal turned to face Mia, who by the narrowed eyes and pinched lips, didn't buy a word of it. How could she with Freddie smiling like an idiot? Before Mia could chastise him, he gave her his most innocent grin. "Want to come with me to take a look at the north rows? I want to check how the fruit set is going today before the rain."

She regarded him for a long second and Cal could just see the fight going on behind her eyes whether to call him out on his ruse or not. It had been a point of contention since he'd got the cast two weeks ago. He was warmed by her concern, but he was not used to being watched over so closely.

"Sure," she said finally and patted the seat next to her. He came around and climbed in. "I know you think I was coming down to spy on you, but I actually need to talk to you."

There was unease in her voice and Cal looked at her. "Of course, what's up?"

"It's about Samuel," Mia said, biting her lip.

Cal straightened, dread building in the pit of his stomach. "What happened?"

Mia's eyes stayed glued to the dirt road. "He came to my office yesterday morning and started questioning our decision to go biodynamic. It was... he was very judgmental... kept saying *we* when talking about the winery. He apologized, but... I don't know... I just don't feel comfortable or even safe with him alone. I'm probably making too much of it..."

"I doubt you are, Mia. I know he's been with the winery a long time, but he isn't irreplaceable. If he makes you feel unsafe, fire him. Or I can do it."

Cal knew that in situations like this it might be helpful for him to come out so he could share his own experiences with men like Samuel. But when he moved away from the central valley, he'd made the decision to live stealth. He was by no means ashamed of being trans. He knew it gave him an incredibly unique perspective in the world, but he wanted to live his life as a man, as he'd always envisioned, and without the complications that came with explaining anything.

Mia let out a heavy sigh as her shoulders sagged. "I'll think more about it. I don't want to lose the extra hands right now," Mia said, pointedly looking down at Cal's cast. The thought of her keeping a man on that she didn't feel comfortable around for his sake didn't sit well.

"We can handle it. Hire some day workers if needed. As for the winemaking part of his job, I've got a degree in that too, remember. I've been making wine alongside my dad since I was fifteen," Cal said.

Mia looked over at him, seemingly considering his idea, but then she gave him a thoughtful frown. "If I do fire him,

I'm gonna need a better reason than I don't like being around him alone."

"He makes you feel unsafe, Mia. That's more than enough reason." Cal thought back to how he acted toward Mia when she came down to bring coffee during the freeze alerts, and the time he'd offered to help with the chicken coop. He had this subtle possessiveness toward Mia, and Cal suspected Samuel had some ill feelings toward him as well because he was hired as manager instead of him.

Mia nodded slowly but didn't say anything. Cal wanted to press the issue, but knew it wasn't his place. He'd said his piece about it and made it clear Mia had his support.

"Hey, after we check the rows, do you want to come up and see what I've found out about our letters?"

It took Cal a second to figure out what Mia was referring to. "Oh, yeah, you were going to tell me what else you found out," Cal said, genuinely excited to hear more about how Adam fit into the picture and what became of Anne.

"Yes, I was, but someone fell out of a tree and I kind of forgot to bring it up again," Mia teased.

They spent a couple of hours going through the rows making sure the tiny self-pollinating flowers were progressing and had no evidence of rot. He was very optimistic about the harvest based on the amount and quality of the cluster. Now if only the weather would cooperate for the next couple of months.

"Ready to head up to the house before we get drenched?" Mia said as the cacophony of big, fat raindrops splattering across the broad grape leaves began to get louder.

They ran to the golf cart and jumped in, Mia laughing as she threw it into gear and hauled ass up to the house. Cal leaned up in his seat to pull up the top panel of the windshield and nearly tumbled out as they hit a muddy patch and slid a little. Mia reached out and grabbed onto his belt loop in an effort to steady him as he finished clicking the panel into place.

He chuckled as his butt slammed back down into the seat. "I'd rather get wet than die, Mia."

"I had a hold of you," Mia countered as she floored it to get up the steep hill to her driveway. She pulled all the way up to the steps and they jumped out, running as the rain pelted down on them.

She opened the door with a flourish and pulled off her muddy boots, setting them in a rubber tray that sat in the entryway. Cal did the same. He stood and looked around, never getting tired of the beautiful architecture and Mission-style furniture.

"I'll get you a towel," Mia said as she turned to look at him. His shirt was soaked through as a result of trying to get the windshield up. *Shit.* "Better yet, come with me. I'll get you a hair dryer for the cast and a dry shirt."

He wanted to argue, but knew he'd sound foolish. He was dripping all over the polished stone floor. He padded behind her, slowing to peek into what he figured was her bedroom. "Guest bathroom is down the hall. You'll find a hair dryer under the sink. I'll bring you a dry shirt."

Cal debated waiting to take off his shirt until Mia brought him the dry one, but he had to get his cast dry before the water permeated it any further. He dug out the hair dryer and plugged it in, then took his shirt off and dropped it into the sink for the time being. As he set the dryer on low and began moving over the cast, he caught his reflection in the mirror.

Until he started transitioning, he never looked at himself. He always knew what he'd see didn't fit. As his body started changing into what he'd always envisioned, he'd spend time looking at himself, noting every change that was bringing him closer to the real him. Now with the body of a man, hair, muscle definition and all, he liked what he saw.

A knock on the door pulled him away from his thoughts and he shut off the dryer. He panicked for a second before seeing a towel hanging behind him. He grabbed it and held it to his chest as if he were in the middle of drying off. He cracked the door open a few inches and reached his casted hand out. "Thanks."

"Welcome. The dryer working on your cast?" Mia asked, pointing to it.

"Oh, yeah. Almost dry. Thanks for letting me use it... and the shirt," he said with a grin. Mia's eyes traveled down to the towel he was holding to his chest, then back up to his shoulders.

"Oh, right. Here." She handed it to him and if Cal wasn't mistaken, he could have sworn there was a slight flush to her cheeks. "I'll take your wet shirt and throw it in the dryer with mine."

"Thanks." He took his shirt out of the sink and handed it to her. "I'll be out in a second," he said as he pulled the shirt close to his chest while still grasping the towel against it.

"Okay, meet me in the kitchen," Mia said, finally turning away.

Cal closed the door softly and put the towel back. He looked at the shirt and then it hit him why Mia seemed slightly flustered. She'd given him one of Tom's shirts. He felt a pang, deep in his chest. He slipped the shirt on—a dark gray, long-sleeve Henley—and was surprised to find it fit perfectly.

He made his way to the kitchen and saw Mia was already at the table, laptop open. She was leaning forward, staring intently at whatever was on the screen. He pulled up a chair next to her and sat down.

"So, I found out that Patty married a man named Adam in 1946." She scrolled to an article, Adam's obituary, and Cal read it.

"Wow, he died on the property." He scratched at his beard and looked at Mia. "Did you find out what happened to Anne?" Mia clicked on another tab and Cal read the story about how she was presumably killed in a plane crash. "Damn." He swiped his thumb under his eye, inexplicably sad about someone he'd never met and by all accounts would have died already by now.

"Yeah, I know," Mia said, voice soft with sympathy. She pointed to the shirt he had on. "That fits you pretty well. You should keep it."

Cal's mouth almost fell open in surprise. "I... I couldn't."

"Why? It was just sitting in a drawer." She gazed down at the shirt once more and she swallowed hard before looking back up to Cal with a soft, sad smile. "I want you to have it."

It felt strange, wearing another man's shirt, especially one who had died—and meant so much to the giver. But he found it impossible to say no. In that moment, he realized it would be very hard to say no to anything Mia asked of him. "Okay. Thank you," he said softly. Her eyes brightened and Cal felt a fluttering in his chest.

"Okay, so, here's the really interesting part I found," Mia said as she turned back to the computer, breaking whatever spell Cal found himself falling into. He refocused and looked at her computer screen as she clicked on two saved images and brought them up side-by-side. "The one on the left is Patty and Adam. The one on the right is Anne."

Cal leaned in close, eyes going back and forth between

the two faces, taking in the eyes, the nose, shape of the lips, size of the ears.

"They must have been siblings, right? But it makes no mention of a sister in his obituary, and they have different surnames," Mia said, voice ebullient with intrigue.

Cal studied the photos some more. Siblings could be the explanation. But Cal had a different theory. One that made his heart leap into his throat at the possibility.

11

Mia stood on her front porch with a wide smile on her face as she saw the silver Prius pull up to the drive. She skipped down the steps as soon as it stopped and watched as a tall, black man with a barrel chest and wide grin unfolded himself from the backseat.

"Girl, it's been a minute," he said as she leaped into his outstretched arms. Her feet lifted off the ground for a moment as he picked her up and squeezed her tight. "How the hell do you get better looking every time I see you? You really are a fine wine."

She shook her head as he let her down gently. "Very funny, Lloyd." She took a few steps back so he could collect his suitcase and tip the driver. "How was the flight? The ride?"

"Short and quiet."

"Just how you like your men," Mia said, ducking her shoulder to avoid a lazy swat from Lloyd.

"You've got jokes, huh?" he said with amused affection.

"Show me to my rooms and then I want the lay of the land. Been a while since I've been here. Is that cute sommelier still here? Joe, was it? He's so fine with that big, shiny beard…"

Mia laughed. Her friend was a hopeless flirt. "Yes, he's still here." Mia bowed and then grabbed his shoulder bag for him as he hefted his suitcase up the stairs. "I'm so glad you are here," she said as she led him down the hall where the guest rooms were.

"Me too." He regarded her with a thoughtful smile when they stopped at his room. "You seem happy."

The observation gave her pause. She'd spent so much time the past year and a half grieving, then being angry, finally settling on sadness and stress as she worked to make sure the winery stayed in the black. She realized that Lloyd was right. She was happy.

"I guess I am," she said with a shrug. "Get settled and meet me in the kitchen. We'll have a snack and chat before I give you a tour."

They spent an hour catching each other up on things they hadn't covered in their weekly phone calls. She told him about the letters Cal had found, and Lloyd agreed that there had to be much more to the story. "You need to try to reach out to the public library, or maybe even one of the Giambi family members. Are they still around here?"

"I have no idea. I guess I could ask the Trasks down the road. They've had their winery longer than the Giambi's, I think."

"You should get Cal to look in the attic again too. Maybe there's more stuff up there. Or even up here," he said, pointing up to the ceiling.

"Maybe I will. He's actually at the doctor's finally getting his cast cut off. I thought he was going to tear it off himself the last two weeks." Mia laughed. She stopped abruptly when Lloyd gave her a knowing smirk.

"Don't tease me, Lloyd. Please." Her words came out more plaintive than she meant, and Lloyd's eyes softened immediately.

"I won't, sweetheart. I'm just happy for you. I can't wait to meet this fella."

"Lloyd, there's nothing going on. He's a good man. He's becoming a friend, I think. But that's it."

Lloyd stayed quiet, reaching to grab a few grapes and pop them into his mouth. Then he picked up his wine glass and took a sip. "Oof, this is good."

"That was the last vintage before we took over." Mia tapped the bottle. In a couple of months, they'd be bottling Tom's first and last harvest. She sighed, wondering how she was going to feel when they started that process.

"Well, I can't wait to taste a Torwood vintage," Lloyd said with a warm smile.

AFTER SCRUBBING ALL THE DEAD SKIN OFF HIS ARM, CAL sighed in relief as he shut off the tap and grabbed a towel. He inspected his slightly atrophic forearm as he dried it. "Not too bad."

He had a list of stuff to get to and was eager to be able to do them all with two functioning hands. Even with his forearm and wrist weak and stiff, it was better than having that damn cast on.

On his way out to the rows, he passed the production room and his thoughts turned to the conversation he'd had with Mia a couple of weeks earlier about Samuel. Nothing had been decided yet, Cal was waiting on Mia to tell him what she wanted to do.

He'd been thinking about what they'd do without his expertise, but Cal felt confident he could do the job. Winemaking was an art as much as it was a skill. It took passion, attention to detail, and above all, patience. What college didn't teach Cal, experience did. He was excited to take this harvest he was cultivating all the way to the bottle.

Still, it was daunting. The winery had a long legacy. They also had vendor contracts that hinged on a quality product. Mia had taken some time to put her faith in his ability to grow top quality grapes. Would it be too much of a gamble for her to trust him with making them into the vineyard's signature wine?

Cal was brought out of his thoughts at the sound of the electric purr of Mia's golf cart. He smiled when he saw her heading toward him, a tall black man sitting next to her. She stopped about five feet from him and jumped out, a wide smile on her face. "Hey Cal. This is my best friend, Lloyd. He's visiting this weekend."

Lloyd unfolded from the seat and ambled over. He held out his hand and Cal gave it a firm shake. Well, as firm as he could, the man's hand swallowed his.

"Nice to meet you, Cal. I've heard a lot about you," Lloyd said with a big grin. Cal's eyes flashed to Mia's as she averted hers, and a rush of warmth moved up his chest. "Okay, maybe *a lot* is an overstatement..." Lloyd amended, probably picking up on Mia's slight discomfort. Either way, Cal was flattered.

"You're the friend from San Francisco," Cal said, remembering Mia had talked about him a couple of times.

"Oh, you know of me?" Lloyd put his hand to his chest and fluttered his eyelashes making Cal laugh. He liked the guy.

Mia chimed in with mild exasperation. "Okay, enough of the awkward introductions. Is it okay if we tag along for a bit? Lloyd would like a little tour."

"Yes, little is the key word. It's too hot and sunny for me down here," he said, fanning himself. "We only get about two weeks of actual sunshine in the Bay Area, and it never gets above seventy-five..."

Mia rolled her eyes and laughed at her friend. "That's such an exaggeration."

Cal grinned and gestured for them to follow him. "Come on, you can help me check on the leaves and clusters."

Cal felt a gentle tap on his shoulder and turned back to see Mia's concerned gaze. "Hey, didn't you just come from your doctor's appointment? How is the arm?"

Cal held it up and rotated it from the elbow as much as he could. "It's healed. I have to take it easy still, but I can use it again, finally."

"How about physical therapy?" she asked.

"Doc gave me some simple exercises I'll do every night before bed, Scout's Honor," he said, holding up three fingers in the Scout's salute.

"Okay, I'll trust you on that," Mia said as she narrowed her eyes.

They walked the rows as Cal inspected the leaves and few remaining flowers as most were dropping off as the berries were taking shape. "So, this yellowing, does it mean the vines need water?" Lloyd asked as he tugged lightly on a leaf.

Cal nodded. "It's a bit dry, yes, but we want the vines to

be a little under stress. It makes the plant concentrate on the fruit, making it better, sweeter."

"Really?" Lloyd said, eyebrows raised in keen interest.

"Yep. When resources are scarce, they put all their energy into their offspring, so to speak."

"Struggle makes the fruit sweeter," Lloyd said as he looked at Mia, a poignant smile on his face. Cal's chest tightened at the unspoken communication between the two. For a moment, it made him long for someone to be close to.

"Thanks for letting us tag along, Cal. We'll let you get back to work. I'm going to take Lloyd up to the tasting room."

"I gotta say hi to that hunky sommelier," Lloyd said with a waggle of his eyebrows.

"Please, ignore him. He still thinks he's twenty-five and single," Mia said as she grabbed Lloyd's hand to lead him back to the golf cart.

"Hey, I am single... ish." Lloyd corrected as he winked at Cal.

"Come on, Lloyd," Mia groaned good-naturedly, making Cal chuckle.

They were almost to the end of the row when Lloyd turned around and yelled. "If you don't have plans, I'm making chicken cacciatore tonight at the house. You should come up."

Cal's eyes widened, and he looked at Mia who shrugged and called out. "He always makes enough to feed an army."

Cal mulled over the invitation for only a few seconds. He'd like to spend more time with the two. He imagined Lloyd might offer up a few stories about Mia too. Cal would really like to know what she was like before she moved down to the central coast and became a winery owner.

"Sure, if you don't mind. Beats me having to cook." Mia's

smile was easy to see even from the forty feet that separated them.

"See you at six, then," she said with a little wave.

He gave them a thumbs up and turned back to the vines, a big, stupid grin spread over his face.

12

"How come you didn't invite Joe?" Mia asked, only half-serious as she checked the pasta.

"Because Joe is as straight as a board. I asked." Lloyd dropped his chin to his chest and stuck out his lower lip in utter disappointment.

"You are something else." Mia shook her head in disbelief.

"I know, I know." He stopped stirring for a moment and turned to Mia, his eyebrows drawn together. "It's okay that I invited Cal, right? I guess I really should have asked."

Mia smiled at her friend and put a hand on his arm. "It's okay." She should be peeved that Lloyd invited Cal to dinner without asking her first, but she couldn't find it in herself to be. Truth be told, she had been delighted that the two seemed to get along right from the start. Cal took Lloyd's theatrics in stride and didn't seem annoyed or offended at his candor. She was looking forward to the two getting to know each other.

"You sure?" His eyes still held a hint of worry and she reached out to squeeze his forearm.

"I'm sure. Please... just don't embarrass me too much," she laughed. She trusted Lloyd to keep her confidence about Cal, but that didn't mean he wouldn't tease her and most likely share some entertaining stories about them in their early days in San Francisco.

"Oh, only a little bit." He flashed her a mischievous smile before turning back to the stove. "He is quite handsome. Sturdy-looking too."

"Sturdy-looking?" Mia chuckled. Then her mind flashed back to seeing Cal shirtless. The towel he was holding up to his chest obscured most of his torso, but from what she saw of his shoulders and upper chest, Lloyd was right. *Very sturdy. And strong.*

"I mean, he's shorter than I pictured... but he looks like he can lift big, heavy things." He made a vague waving gesture with the hand that wasn't holding the wooden spoon.

"So, your type then?" Mia teased.

"Oh, certainly, but something tells me he doesn't bat for my team." Before Mia could respond, there was a knock on the kitchen door. "Oh, he even knows to come to the side door?" Lloyd said with a wink.

Mia rolled her eyes as she walked to the door. "Hey," she said with a crooked smile as she opened it.

"Hi. Thanks again for inviting me for dinner," Cal said, handing her a bottle of wine. "Thought this would go nice with what we're having."

"Perfect. Thanks, Cal." She took it to the counter, then grabbed the corkscrew out of the drawer and held it out toward him. "Want to do the honors?"

"Well, you clean up nice," Lloyd said as he glanced at Cal before returning his attention to the stove. With the exception of his interview, Mia had only seen him in cargo pants, work shirts, heavy boots, and a baseball cap. She took in his dark jeans, charcoal short-sleeved button up, and Chelsea boots. It even looked like he put some effort into styling his short hair. She ignored the flutter low in her stomach.

"Thank you, Lloyd," Cal said with a half-grin as he opened the wine, setting it on the counter to let it breathe. "Is there anything I can do to help?"

"How about helping Mia set the table? I'm pretty much done here." Lloyd removed the pot from the burner and shut off the stove.

"I'll grab wine glasses, can you get the plates, Cal?" Mia said as she walked to the cabinet by the sink and Cal turned to open the cabinet next to the stove. Lloyd looked at Mia, eyebrows raised halfway up his forehead. She gave him a stern look, silently warning him not to comment that Cal seemed to know his way around her kitchen. "Meet you in the dining room, Cal," she said, ignoring Lloyd's pleased-as-punch smirk.

"How long have you known Lloyd?" Cal asked as he laid the plates out.

"Oh well, I met him when I moved to San Francisco when I was twenty-one. The first week, in fact. I met him before I even met Tom." She smiled fondly remembering her first impression of the tall, sassy but sweet, gay man. She'd grown up in a conservative mid-western town, and the city—it had been a very big culture shock.

"How did you meet?" Cal asked.

"Oh, I tell it best, dear. I'll give you all kinds of stories about this one here," Lloyd said as he set down a large serving dish and then walked back into the kitchen.

Cal looked at Mia and gave her a soft smile. "Can't wait to hear some of them. I'll get the wine."

As both men disappeared into the kitchen, she thought how surreal it was having Cal over for a dinner that wasn't the extension of a work-related event. It was also the first time she'd entertained guests since before Tom had passed. She found herself really looking forward to the night and to getting to know Cal outside of work. She pushed away the tendril of guilt she felt at the thought.

"Let's eat!" Lloyd announced as he came back into the dining room with a large, steaming serving dish. Cal came out with the side dish and the bottle of wine he brought. He poured a little into Mia and Lloyd's glasses, placed the bottle on the table, and looked at Mia with an expectant grin. "Let me know what you think."

Mia brought the glass to her nose, took it away, swirled it and brought it back. "I smell raspberry, a hint of strawberry... plum?" She smiled as Cal nodded.

"What else?" he asked as he tucked his hands behind his back and leaned forward.

She swirled it again and inhaled through her nose and mouth. "Vanilla... anise... fennel." She finally brought it to her lips and took a healthy amount into her mouth, swishing it around for a few seconds before swallowing. "It's really good. Light, nice and dry. Tannins aren't overpowering. I really like it."

Lloyd echoed Mia's words. "Yeah, I love the lightness. Where's it from?" he asked as he picked up the bottle and looked at the label.

"Remember during my interview I told you I spent a year in the Willamette Valley with Marcus Rey at his Touchstone Vineyard? He called me back a year and a half later to oversee the production of the harvest." His grin was not so much cocky as it was amused.

Mia leaned back in her chair, surprised and deeply

impressed. "Is this your way of telling me you can also take on the winemaking side?"

Cal shrugged, "Yes, I suppose so."

"Suppose so? Man, you are smooth." Lloyd raised his glass and dipped his head toward him, a wide grin on his face. His eyes turned toward Mia. "Now you can finally get rid of that cretin, Samuel."

A flash of surprise came over Cal's face, but he recovered quickly. He sat down, poured himself some wine and refilled Mia and Lloyd's glasses.

Mia pulled the chicken cacciatore toward her and gestured for Cal to give her his plate. "I think maybe I should have a talk with him first?"

"I don't think that's a good idea," Cal and Lloyd said in unison. They looked up at each other as Mia's eyes went from Cal's to Lloyd's.

Cal shifted in his seat. "Guys like Samuel... they don't usually respond well... to verbal warnings—"

"By women," Lloyd interrupted, his tone reflecting the indignation he obviously felt on Mia's behalf. "Based on what you've told me about him, he's a misogynistic, egotistical asshole who seems to think he has some sort of ownership over you and the winery."

Cal sighed and nodded slowly. "The last thing I want to do is tell you how to deal with him, but in my experience"—he stopped himself and ran a hand over his beard—"witnessing men like that with women... they don't listen and they certainly don't learn."

Mia regarded him for a moment, wanting to know the circumstances behind that statement. What he said was disheartening, but she knew it was true. "Well, we can talk about it later. I don't want our dinner conversation to revolve around business," Mia said, mustering a smile as she finished dishing out the chicken.

"That's right. On to much more pleasant things, like how we met," Lloyd said with a gleeful grin as he looked at Mia.

She rolled her eyes. "Please, go on..." she said as she tucked into her meal.

Cal did the same and hummed enthusiastically at the first bite. "Wow, this is great."

"Thank you. It's one of my simpler dishes, but Mia loves it," Lloyd said with an affectionate smile. "So, how we met... let's see, it was... how old are you now?" Lloyd asked, his voice teeming with mirth.

She'd never been self-conscious about her age, but she didn't want it announced in front of Cal. "You know darn well how old I am."

"Right... so that would make it... twenty-one years ago. Exactly half your life." Lloyd winked. She narrowed her eyes at him, but he ignored it. "It was my first day as a line cook at this little, old, greasy diner where Mia was doing the books for the owner. It was your first job out of school, right?"

"Yep. I'd just moved to the city, thinking I was going to land this cushy accounting job straight away. Boy, was I naïve." She chuckled. She remembered those early days, the shock of the cost of living, but the joy at being in a place where everyone was so different.

"Well, it didn't take long for you to become my favorite person." He turned to Cal. "I was standing near the kitchen door, getting ready to learn the ropes, when this huge white man sitting at the counter points at me and yells, "You better be wearing gloves when you cook my food, boy."

Mia remembered that day so vividly. She'd left her conservative town because of behavior like that, and when she'd heard the man say that from her office off the kitchen, she wasn't going to let it stand.

"I was kind of shocked into silence, but here comes this woman, all five foot three of her." He pointed to Mia. "She got right in his face and told him that wasn't tolerated in their establishment and to leave."

Cal's eyes widened as he looked at Mia. His smile was full of admiration. "Good for you, Mia. That was brave."

"Yeah, well, it also got her fired. I felt so bad, even though it wasn't my fault. I went outside during my first break and found you out in the alley, leaning against the wall, wiping furiously at your eyes. You remember what I told you?"

"Stop rubbing, sweetie, you're smearing your mascara?"

Lloyd rolled his eyes. "After that..."

"You told me for a white girl, I'm pretty cool and said we were going to be great friends."

"I did, and I was right on both counts." Lloyd looked at Cal and his eyes grew soft and earnest. "She's the best friend I've ever had, and I'd fight a bear for her." Without looking away from Cal he pointed to Mia who had tears building in her eyes. "Don't rub, sweetie."

MIA LEANED HER FOREARMS ON THE PORCH RAILING, TAKING IN the full moon as she watched Cal walk down the hill to the barn.

"I like him," Lloyd said as he came to join her.

A smile spread over her lips before she reigned it back in and looked at Lloyd. "He's a good guy."

"And that crush you have on him? It is most certainly not one way."

She stood and turned to lean her back on the railing. "I'm forty-two. I don't have a 'crush,'" she refuted, but it sounded halfhearted, even to her own ears. She tilted her head up, eyes landing on the joists holding the porch roof up. She sighed, resigned yet deeply curious. "How can you tell?"

"His eyes barely left you the whole night. He really listened when I was regaling him with stories about your time in San Francisco." Lloyd's voice went down an octave. "He helped with the dishes." He crossed his arms over his chest and gave her a self-satisfied smirk. "He likes you."

"I don't know what to think about all this, Lloyd. I know Tom's been gone for nearly two years, but... I don't know... I never thought I'd be interested in someone else, you know? Let alone someone I hired to work at the winery."

"You know what Tom told me the first time I met him?"

Mia faced Lloyd, eyebrows drawn together. "No. What did he say?"

"He said that even if you didn't choose him, he just wanted you to be happy."

Mia's hand went to her mouth as a sob bubbled up unexpectedly. She'd forgotten she had been kind of seeing another man when she'd met Tom. She'd never told him that the moment she met him, she knew he was the one. "He said that?" Her voice cracked as she tried to hold in her emotions.

"He did." Lloyd smiled and leaned in to swipe a thumb under her eye. "I can't help but think he would say the same thing if he were standing here right now."

"If he were standing here now, we wouldn't be having this conversation," Mia pointed out as she drew in a breath. As her tears subsided, she realized that what she had said didn't hurt as much as she thought it would.

She turned back around in time to see Cal's silhouette blend into the darkness near the bottom of the hill. Could she be happy with someone other than Tom? Truly happy? She couldn't answer that question at that moment, but she could promise herself that she would leave it open.

PART 4: VERAISON

13

Cal looked up as he heard Mia stop at the top of one of the rows with a small group of women taking a tour. "The biggest explosion of growth happens around this time... it's called veraison. It's when the chlorophyll green starts to disappear, and the grapes start turning their respective colors—yellowish hues for white wines and red and purple for red wines."

Cal smiled at the practiced words that Mia had gone over with him after she'd had the idea of giving wine tours a few times a month as part of their newly developed VIP wine tasting package. She had added it to their website less than three weeks ago, and she was already booked out through the next two months.

The smile faded as he saw Samuel approach the group. He stood slightly behind Mia until she had no choice but to acknowledge him. "And this is Samuel, one of our winemakers." Cal couldn't see Samuel's face, but he could see his spine stiffen at Mia's introduction.

Still, he stepped even closer to Mia and addressed the group, explaining how to tell when the grapes are ready for harvest. He started throwing out all the technical terms and instruments they used to measure acidity and sugar. Every time Mia tried to interject, he'd talk over her.

Cal wondered if he should step in, but he didn't want to do the very thing that Samuel was doing, taking over her tour. He stopped working and watched—growing more annoyed with the man on Mia's behalf as he continued to drone on in front of the guests.

He was about to call Samuel over under the guise of needing help when Mia was finally able to cut him off. "Thanks for taking the time to explain that process, Samuel." She turned to her group. "Now, if you'll follow me, I'll introduce you to our vineyard manager."

Cal walked to the end of the row to meet them, all the while keeping an eye on Samuel. The expression on his face as he watched Mia walk away from him chilled Cal to the bone. He was going to have to say something to Mia.

Cal grinned as he caught eyes with Mia. "Ladies, this is Cal Sanders. He manages the vineyard."

Cal dipped his head in greeting and spent a few moments answering questions before Mia ushered them back up the hill to the tasting room. As he was walking back to where he was thinning out a few heavy clusters, he was stopped by Samuel calling his name out sharply. "You sure have Mia snowed, don't you?"

He faced him, trying to hide the anger he felt bubbling up. "What is that supposed to mean?" He asked in an even tone.

"You come in here, making all these changes to the vineyard. You're in her office all the time too. And I know you went up to dinner at her house a few times. She just lost her husband, have some respect." Samuel spat out as he stepped closer, trying to intimidate Cal with his height.

"I've done nothing to the vineyard without discussing it with Mrs. Torwood first and getting her approval. As for your implication, I suggest you take your own advice."

Anything Cal said further would be used to fuel the fire of Samuel's entitlement and anger, so he turned away, refusing to engage with him.

"I know your game, Sanders. And I'm sure as hell not going to let you take advantage of Mia."

Cal kept walking, jaw clenched and eyes narrowed. He didn't know what Samuel was capable of, but it was probably in everyone's best interest if they didn't find out.

Mia waved goodbye to the tour group and walked around the tasting room bar and grabbed herself a bottle of water. "How are the tours going?" Joe asked as he wiped down the section of the bar a couple of wine tasters had recently left.

"Good. It's tiring though. Who knew talking and walking expended so much energy?" Mia chuckled.

Joe nodded. "I remember when I used to do them for the winery I used to work at. It isn't as easy as it looks."

Mia finished her water bottle and tossed it into the recycling bin. "Well, I'm glad I only do it a few times a month. I'll see you later, Joe. Have a good rest of your day."

"Thanks, Mrs. Torwood. You too."

Mia stepped outside and stretched her back, surprised the sun was already starting to set. She looked out at the outdoor seating area with the new string lights and planters they'd just put in to give it a more welcoming ambiance. They'd be hosting their first ever grape stomping event in a couple of months and even though it was going to take a ton of work and planning, she was really looking forward to it.

When Tom had died and she realized she had to stay at the winery and make it work, she'd been so angry. Even though she had started to settle into their new life, growing fond of the land, Tom's death had wiped that all away. But then she'd hired Cal.

Now, she was not only fond of it, she was growing to love it. Even having Lloyd visit and reminiscing about the old times, she realized she didn't want to move back anymore. The vineyard was her home now, and she knew seeing it through Cal's eyes had a lot to do with that.

She heard the back door to the tasting room open and close, and turned to see Samuel walking toward her. *Great. Is he following me today?*

"Hi, Mia. Thanks for letting me butt in today. It was fun to talk about the winemaking process with our tour guests," he said with a wide smile as he came to stand next to her.

She subtly took a step back as she mentally cringed at him saying *our* tour guests. "Yes, I appreciate you taking the time out of your busy schedule to talk to them."

He dipped his head, a smile still on his face. "Are you heading back to your office now? I wanted to talk to you about something, but I didn't want others to overhear."

Mia was about to head down in her golf cart back to her office and figured that would be as safe a place as any. There would still be a few workers around, she'd be the one driving and the distance they had to go was relatively short. God, was she really thinking about an escape plan if Samuel tried something? Was she being too paranoid? She shook off the thought, but not the inclination to be on the safe side.

"We can take my golf cart down and talk," she said as

she started to walk toward it, leaving him no other choice but to follow.

"I can drive us down," he said as they approached it.

"I've got it," she said, veering over to the driver's side and getting in. He slowly slipped in beside her and immediately grabbed onto the roof. She just kept from rolling her eyes as she backed out of the spot and pulled onto the smooth dirt road that led down the hill.

"What did you need to speak to me about?" she said, polite but dispassionate.

"It's about Cal." He turned to look at her, a placating look on his face. "I know you think he's doing a good job, but I think he has some bad intentions toward you. I think you need to fire him."

Mia's eyes went wide as she slowed the cart. "Excuse me?"

The muscles in Samuel's jaw bunched. "He has undue influence over you in regard to the winery. He wants to take it over, and he's trying to seduce you into letting him do it."

Mia stared at Samuel, trying to comprehend what had just come out of his mouth. The unease she felt being around him ratcheted up to fear. The man was delusional.

"Samuel. I have no idea where you got that idea, but it is patently untrue. Furthermore, I don't need to explain the way I run *my* winery, who *I* hire, or how I interact with *my* employees to anyone."

He held up his hand, a conciliatory look on his face. "Of course you don't, Mia. But you aren't a man, and you can't see what I see—"

Mia stomped on the cart's brake, making them both lurch forward even though they were crawling along at that point. "I'm going to stop you right there. Being a woman has nothing to do with what I can and can't see. I told you what you said was untrue. That's the end of it. I don't want to hear another word about it. You have no business, and you have no right, got it?"

Mia looked at him, and he faced forward, giving her his profile. His jaw was clenched and his eyes, glassy with rage. His hand, still hanging onto the roof, was white from how tightly he gripped it. Her gaze fell to the corded muscles of his forearm shifting under his skin. He was vibrating with such vicious energy Mia thought he might strike her.

Before she could decide what to do, he burst out of the seat and then slowly turned to face Mia. His eyes, lost in rage seconds before, became cold and impassive. It was terrifying. "I got it."

CAL STOPPED STRUMMING HIS GUITAR AND COCKED HIS HEAD when he thought he heard a knock on his door. When it came again, this time louder, he put the guitar down and walked to the door, wondering who it could be. "Mia," he said, surprised and then concerned when he saw she'd been crying.

"Sorry to come over unannounced, but I just had an encounter with Samuel," she said, sniffling and wiping at her still moist eyes.

Cal ushered her in and closed the door. "What happened, Mia? Did he hurt you?" Cal asked, heart thundering hard in his chest.

"No, he didn't hurt me. He was up at the tasting room and asked if he could talk to me privately. I told him I was going back to the office, so he rode with me down in the cart." She took a seat on the couch and Cal grabbed a box of tissues from the kitchen counter and set it on the coffee table before taking a seat next to her. She regarded him for a long moment, a hesitant look on her face.

"Mia, what is it? Are you sure he didn't hurt you?"

"I'm sure. He accused you of trying to..." She stopped and closed her eyes, shaking her head slowly. She pushed out a breath. "Of trying to seduce me to gain control of the winery. When I told him he was wrong and never to bring something like that up again, he got really angry... like a silent rage. I was actually scared he would do something." Mia pulled another tissue out of the box and wiped at her eyes. She looked at Cal who had his head down and a grim look on his face. "You don't look surprised."

"He essentially accused me of the same thing right to my face. Told me he was going to do something about it." God, what if he had hurt her? Cal would never forgive himself. "I'm sorry, I should have come to you immediately. If I had..."

Mia put a hand on Cal's knee. "Hey, it's okay. It's over now. I'm going to call him into my office tomorrow first thing and fire him."

"If you want someone else present Mia, I can be there or send up Freddie and Grady. They can escort him out right after you fire him."

Mia took in a deep breath and then let it out slowly. "I think you'll set him off if you are there. I'd feel better if Freddie and Grady were close." Cal could see the tension in her jaw, the unease in her eyes.

"I'll have them go up shortly before he's due to arrive. If he says or tries to do anything, Freddie and Grady will be right there. I'll be nearby," Cal said, trying to sound reassuring. He wished he could do this for her, but she was the owner and employer.

"Okay," Mia said shakily.

Cal hated to see her so shaken. He glanced at his watch and saw it was nearing seven o'clock. "Have you had something to eat? I could fix us some grilled cheese sandwiches?"

She looked down at her watch as well and bit her lip, considering the offer. "You know what, that sounds good. Sure."

"Yeah?" Cal said, a little surprised she'd said yes. The line between employee and employer felt like it had been blurred between them a while back, but Cal never really thought about to what degree. Were they friends now? Or just friendly?

"Can I help?" she asked as he got up and put his guitar back on its stand in the corner of the living room.

"Nah. Have a seat and relax," he said as he went about grabbing all the ingredients and cookware he needed.

"Sometimes I hear you play when I'm working late in the office. You're pretty good," Mia said as she came over and sat at the bar on the other side of the kitchen counter.

"Oh, thanks. I'm a bit rusty right now. Trying to get my wrist and forearm back in shape." He mimicked fingering the guitar fretboard with his left hand.

"Ah, I guess that would affect your playing."

"It's not too bad, though. Just takes time and patience."

He made quick work of the sandwiches and cut up a couple of apples and they ate right there at the bar.

"I was thinking I'd give those letters to the WASP Museum in Texas. They really give a great account of what it was like to be in the training program. I'll leave that last letter out, though," Mia said after swallowing the last bite of her sandwich. Cal was still on his first half.

"That's a great idea. I wonder though... Are Patty and Adam's kids still alive? I mean, I guess they'd be close to their seventies, but... maybe they'd want to see them first?"

"I suppose I can reach out to the realtor who sold us the winery. They should still have their contact information. Though, I'm pretty sure it was the grandkids who sold it."

Cal started in on his second half before responding. "I think it's worth a go. Maybe they know something about the letters or about their grandmother's relationship to Anne?"

Mia's eyes lit up. "You know Lloyd is almost as invested in this story as us. He said I should check all the attic spaces of both the barn and house for more clues." Mia laughed.

"I'm down if you are." Cal shrugged.

"I'll get in contact with Marsha next week and see what happens. I guess in the meantime we can go scavenging around."

"Sounds good. I am thoroughly intrigued," Cal said. He hadn't voiced his suspicions to Mia yet. He was actually hesitant to do so. What if she reacted in a manner that led Cal to believe she wasn't as open-minded as he hoped she'd be? He didn't want to admit to himself why that would be so important to him. He didn't want to admit a few things to himself when it came to Mia.

14

Mia paced in her office as she waited for Grady and Freddie to show up. It was eight forty-five and Samuel would be there in fifteen minutes.

When she'd called Samuel an hour ago and asked him to come to her office for a meeting, he'd insisted she tell him what it was about. He sounded on edge and annoyed, so Mia had finally told him it was about what he'd said the day before. She left it vague, but she had a feeling Samuel had thought she was coming around and was actually calling him in to discuss firing Cal.

There was a knock on the door, and she breathed out a sigh of relief before moving quickly to the door and opening it. Her heart nearly stopped when she saw only Samuel standing on the landing. "Hi, Mia. Hope you don't mind if I'm a little early. I forgot I had someone coming in to look at one of the de-stemming machines."

Fuck. She ran through ways to stall as she stood there, regarding him silently. He had a casual smile on his face and his eyes were bright and held an air of anticipation. Not a trace of the fury he displayed a mere thirteen hours ago.

But of course not. He thought he was getting his way. That fear she felt when she first opened the door turned into anger. Anger that this man thought he could tell her what to do. Anger that she had to have her employees stand by her because she didn't feel safe firing him.

"Come in. This will only take a moment."

CAL WAS IN THE ROWS PRUNING SOME OVERGROWTH WHEN Freddie came ambling up. "Hey, Jefe, does Mrs. Torwood still need us?" Cal looked up at him and then pushed his glove up to look at his watch. It was eight fifty.

"Yes, you were supposed to be there five minutes ago," Cal said as dread pooled in his stomach. He put his clippers in the holder on his belt and walked toward him.

"I saw Samuel go in already, so I thought…"

Cal's blood ran cold. "Samuel's in her office? Is Grady up there?"

"No, he was waiting for me to come ask you."

"Goddamn it, Freddie!" Cal shouted at the confused man as he took off down the hill. He pulled his phone out of his back pocket, grimacing when his arm caught on something sharp. He ignored it and brought up Mia's number with one hand and hit the call button. It was hard to hear the ringing over his own heavy breathing as he sprinted down the dirt path. He shoved the phone back in his pocket when it went to voicemail.

"Fuck," he growled as he neared the barn and saw no sign of Mia or Samuel. He took the stairs up two at a time, and once on the landing stopped and put his ear to the door. He didn't want to burst in like some over-protective, half-cocked idiot. When he didn't hear anything, he knocked. It was hard, and he tried not to rattle the thing in its hinges.

"Come in," Mia said loudly. He yanked the door open, chest heaving and eyes searching before finding Mia standing behind her desk, leaning on the low filing cabinet. Samuel was sitting in the chair opposite the desk, face flush.

"Sorry to interrupt," Cal said. He offered nothing else as his brain rapidly tried to assess what had been going on in the moments before he knocked. Mia appeared to be uneasy yet unharmed and Samuel looked like he was about to explode at any second.

"It's okay. Samuel was just about to leave," Mia said slowly. Cal noted that Mia was not moving from her spot against the filing cabinet. Her face was impassive, but Cal could see fear mixed with relief in her eyes. He'd gotten there in time, thank God.

He turned his attention to Samuel. He'd never been in a physical altercation with anyone, not since transitioning. He sized Samuel up, thinking he had a better center of gravity and maybe about fifteen pounds on Samuel. Why did he never take those self-defense classes he had been meaning to for years?

Samuel was rooted to the chair, continuing to stare at Mia. "Your husband would be so angry with you, whoring yourself out to the likes of that sorry excuse for a man."

Mia's eyes widened at Samuel's abhorrent words and Cal made a step forward. "Mrs. Torwood said you were leaving. I suggest you do that right now." What he really wanted to do was punch the guy's teeth out, but that would only get him arrested or worse. He looked at Mia for a signal on how to proceed. He really didn't want to have to wrestle the man out of the office.

"Oh, you suggest? What are you gonna do?" he mocked as he stood, his eyes never leaving Mia.

"I'll do whatever it is I need to." He pulled his phone out and called Freddie. "You and Grady get up here to Mrs. Torwood's office right now." He ended the call before Freddie could ask questions. He was still fuming at him for not following his directions earlier.

Finally, Samuel's attention broke from Mia and focused on Cal. "Not man enough to throw me out on your own, huh?" He let out a dark, derisive laugh. "Hell of a boy you picked, Mia."

Cal knew he was trying to goad him into a physical altercation. Cal wouldn't play into his stupid display of machismo. When he heard his guys coming up the stairs, he reached behind him and opened the door. "Samuel has been fired and needs to be removed from the premises. Escort him straight to his car, nowhere else, do you understand?"

Freddie nodded sharply, a contrite look in his eyes. "Yes, of course, Jefe." Grady, with his hulking frame, stepped all the way into the room and crossed his arms over his chest and glared at Samuel. Seemed like there was no love lost between him and Samuel either.

Samuel gave one last look to Mia and then turned back to Cal. "You're going to run this winery into the ground, and I ain't comin' back to save it." He shouldered past Freddie and gave Grady a wide berth as he made his way to the door and yanked it open. Both Freddie and Grady hastened to follow him.

Cal called out to Freddie as he was halfway down the stairs. "Do not let him go anywhere else but straight to his car. Tell him we'll send any personal effects to his house."

"Got it, Jefe. Sorry... about earlier," he said.

"We'll talk about it when you get him off the property," Cal said and then went back to Mia who was now sitting at her desk, head in her hands. Cal could see from the doorway she was shaking.

"I swear if you hadn't got here when you did..." Mia looked up, eyes red and brimming with tears. Cal went to her side of the desk and squatted next to her.

"I'm so sorry I wasn't explicit with Freddie and Grady." Cal was still frustrated at his employees, but he could have been clearer.

"No, it isn't your fault. I told you not to let them know ahead of time what was going on."

"Still, they should have been here."

"How did you know to come?" Mia asked as she dabbed at her eyes.

"Well, Freddie found me in the rows and asked if they were still needed since Samuel was already in your office." Cal reached out and put a hand on her arm. "Are you okay? He didn't try anything, did he?"

"No, he was just saying these awful things. But I think he was going to... he'd gotten up out of his seat and then stopped when we heard you running up the stairs." She gave him a watery, grateful smile and put her hand over his that was on her arm. She pulled it away though, a look of concern on her face when it came away bloody. "Cal?" He looked down at his hand and saw blood.

"Ah, I think I caught my arm on something when I was running through the rows." He gingerly folded up his sleeve, following the trail of blood until he saw a moderately deep gouge right below his elbow. It was still bleeding, but it was sluggish. He took out the handkerchief he always carried in his pocket and pressed it to the wound.

"I have a first aid kit." Mia bent down and opened her

bottom desk drawer and pulled out a red box. She opened it and got out the Betadine, some gauze squares, steri-strips, and a bandaid.

"I can clean it," Cal said as he reached for the Betadine.

"I'll do it for you," she said, and Cal nodded seeing that it was probably a good distraction from thinking about what had happened. What could have happened with Samuel. "Grab the trash can." Cal hid an amused grin and did as he was told. It was not the appropriate time to acknowledge the thrill he got at Mia being bossy. "Hold your arm over it." Cal did as he was told again, and Mia opened the bottle and held it above his arm. "You're not going to scream, are you?" She smirked.

Cal shrugged and played along, glad that Mia seemed okay, playful even. "I might." He cleared his throat, realizing how that sounded. He soldiered on though, shaking himself and gave her a mock-serious nod. "I'm ready, doc."

She poured a liberal amount of the stinging liquid directly on the wound and Cal winced. Mia gave an impressed hum and used one of the gauze pads to clean off the remaining blood that surrounded the wound. She neatly affixed the steri-strips, pulling the wound closed. "I already figured I couldn't get you to go to urgent care, so..."

"You figured right," Cal said as Mia wrapped the wound with gauze and secured it with some tape. When she was done, he rolled his sleeve back down and gave her a warm smile. "Thanks for patching me up, Mia."

"No problem. Stop getting hurt on my vineyard, okay? You're going to make my insurance premiums go up." She smiled as she stood and put the garbage can back where it was.

"I'll try my best." He headed to the door, but Mia stopped him with a hand on his arm.

"Thank you for getting here when you did."

Cal's heart stuttered at the look in Mia's eyes. He had the overwhelming urge to wrap her up in his arms and tell her how fucking terrified he was when he realized she was up here alone with that man. That he'd always be there for her.

"You're welcome. I'm glad you are all right and that he will no longer be here to bother you."

Mia opened her mouth as if to speak but stopped and looked down at the carpet. When she looked up again, she had a smile on her face and her eyes were slightly wider than normal. "Yeah, me too. Guess I'm looking at Torwood's new winemaker now. Let me know if you need to hire extra help."

"Oh, I think I can manage. Freddie and Grady know they are in the dog house. I'm gonna work them really hard for the next couple of weeks."

"Don't be too hard on them," Mia said as she released his arm. He hadn't realized she still had a hold of it. He felt the loss of warmth immediately.

"I'll try not to." Cal smiled, but he was still upset they didn't just do as he'd asked. If Freddie hadn't come and checked though... He didn't want to think about that. "See you later?" He wanted to stay and make sure she was all right, but he didn't want to overstep. Even though he felt like their interactions the last couple of months already had. His thoughts about her certainly had.

She smiled and Cal saw a hint of eagerness in her eyes. "Yeah, that... that would be good if you stopped in later."

He nodded and turned to head to the door, but then paused. His cheeks felt warm at the thought of Mia wanting him to stop in and check on her. "You want to maybe order us some sandwiches for lunch? We can talk more about goats or Patty and Adam and Anne..."

Her smile widened until the corner of her eyes crinkled and Cal couldn't help but grin as well. "That would be great. Meet you back here at noon?"

"You bet." Cal took the steps two at a time as a wide grin spread over his face. He seemed to be doing that a lot lately. When he got to the bottom of the stairs, Freddie was walking back from the parking lot.

"Jefe, I'm so sorry. I didn't realize what was happening, but Grady and I should have been where you told us to be. Is Mrs. Torwood okay?"

"She is. I want you and Grady to be on the lookout though and tell me or Mia immediately if you see Samuel back or even around the property. Understand?"

"Of course. He was saying some pretty nasty things about Mrs. Torwood." Freddie stuffed his hands in his pocket and looked down at the ground. "And you. I know none of it's true… but he was really mad. He threatened to burn the place down."

Cal closed his eyes and clenched his jaw for a second before blowing out a breath. "Thanks for letting me know, Freddie."

Cal headed back to work, wondering just how serious of a threat it was. He imagined a vineyard-wide meeting was needed. Maybe even a call to the police. Looked like talk of goats and Giambi family history would have to wait.

PART 5: HARVEST

15

It had been three weeks since Samuel was fired, and to Mia's relief, there had been no sign of him. She hoped it stayed that way. Veraison was in full swing and there was a growing excitement in the air as the harvest season was quickly approaching.

The previous year's harvest season was hard for Mia as it was the first anniversary of Tom's death. She'd spent a lot of time trying not to think of the vineyard and how the grapes were coming along. She'd left everything up to Jose as she continued work on getting the tasting room remodeled, getting the books in order, and learning how to run and manage the daily operating budget.

She didn't want any grape stomping events or any special celebrations that came with the wine grape harvest. She let Jose oversee everything.

This year was different, though. She was excited to watch the grapes ripen, and she had already told Cal she wanted to learn the process of figuring out when to harvest. And with Samuel gone, she felt lighter, unencumbered by fear and worry.

She had also found some time to track down one of the Giambi grandchildren, Megan, who lived only thirty minutes away. She had told Cal as soon as she set up an appointment with her but was on the fence about inviting him to come along. She wasn't sure if it would be appropriate, being that it had nothing to do with his job.

She thought back to when she was alone with Samuel in her office, right after she'd told him he was fired. He'd started accusing her of leading him on. He railed about how he deserved to take over as manager, not Cal, and how she should have chosen him both for the job and as a potential love interest.

She'd been stunned into silence, and when he'd grown quiet and stood from his chair, Mia knew she was in trouble. But then she'd heard the pounding of footsteps on the stairs, and she nearly sobbed with relief. Cal had knocked, and she'd found her voice. When Cal had burst into her office, his face had been ashen and his eyes wide. His heavy breathing indicated he'd run, and run hard from the rows where he had been working.

Mia wanted to run and hug him right then and there, but she could imagine what Samuel would have done. And when Cal comforted her after Samuel had been escorted out, it made Mia feel seen and safe and cared for—it had been a long time since she'd felt that. And it had felt really good. Especially when she realized she wanted to do the same for Cal.

CAL TOOK HIS HAT OFF AND PULLED OUT HIS HANDKERCHIEF, wiping the sweat from his forehead and eyes. August on the central coast wasn't as brutal as it was in the central valley, but it was still hot. He'd been going through the rows plucking grapes and checking them for seed color and skin texture. He'd invited Mia to join him when she was done with her morning meetings with wine vendors.

"Geez, it's already eighty degrees, and it isn't even noon yet," Mia said as she came strolling up the row with a floppy hat and sun umbrella.

"Yeah, gonna be a hot one. Nice umbrella." He smiled.

"Hey, I gotta keep this fair skin protected," she said as she patted her cheek. She came to stand next to him and angled the umbrella so it would cover him in shade as well. "You, sir, need to be applying sunscreen more often. You'll be thankful when you are my age."

"I'm not that far behind you." Cal chuckled. "But I'll take your advice," he said as he stuffed his handkerchief back in his pocket and put his hat back on. "Ready to eat some grapes?"

They spent close to an hour walking through the rows, picking grapes, chewing them up and then studying the seeds. "You want to see no trace of green in the seeds and the skin to have a nice silky feel on the outside and slightly gritty when you smash it in your palm." Cal told Mia.

"So, based on what you've told me, we're nearly ready for harvest?"

"I'll take a few grapes to test, but yeah, I say another week, maybe two to be on the safe side…" He regarded her closely, remembering that her husband had died during their first harvest. He imagined this was a hard time of year for her.

"Okay, great. It'll be perfect timing for our grape stomping event," she said with a pleased smile.

"My family used to have them too. They are a lot of fun and an excellent revenue generator," Cal said.

"Yeah, hopefully I can pull it off. This will be my first one, attending and organizing." Her smile was bittersweet as she turned to look toward the area in front of the tasting room where the event would be held.

"I'll gladly lend a hand," Cal said earnestly.

"I'm counting on it." Mia's eyes narrowed as she reached up toward Cal's mouth. His first instinct was to pull away, but he stayed still as Mia plucked something from the side of his mustache. "Stranded seed." Mia laughed and wiped it on her pant leg.

Cal ran a hand self-consciously over his face as he felt it flush. "When I first started growing my facial hair out, it was alarming how much food got stuck in it."

Mia cocked her head to the side and then to the other, studying Cal. "I'm trying to picture you without facial hair."

Cal shrugged. "I look about ten years younger."

"Tom tried to grow a beard once. I made him shave it off because it was too patchy and scratchy." Cal tried to hide his surprise at Mia bringing up her husband, but she did it so casually. The wistful smile stayed as she pointed to Cal's face. "Well, I'll always let you know if I see anything that doesn't belong there."

"That's a true friend," Cal said before thinking. Realizing what he'd just implied, his gaze fell to a cluster of grapes as he kicked himself for sounding presumptuous.

"I think we've become friends... wouldn't you say?" Mia's tone was light and reassuring. It made Cal smile and his heart soar.

"I would." Cal agreed. If he had to put a name to how much they've interacted outside of normal work situations and how much they've shared with each other—the word *friend* definitely came to mind.

"Okay. Good." Mia smiled. "Well, friend, how would you

like to accompany me to that meeting I have with Megan Howe tomorrow after work?"

Cal's eyes lit up. "I'd really like that."

Mia stepped up to the door of the sleek, modern single-story house and knocked. It immediately set off a cacophony of sound: a dog barking, a bird squawking an unintelligible word repeatedly, followed by a young child's excited screeching.

She turned to Cal whose eyes were probably as big as hers. "Maybe I should have called when we pulled up." Mia laughed. The door opened and Mia readied an apology, but the woman was laughing as she waved them in.

"Sorry about that. Rest assured, no one could ever sneak into our house unannounced. I'm Megan. I can assume you are Mia and Cal?" She said as she stuck out the hand that wasn't holding back a medium-sized, black, wire-haired dog. Mia took it and shook and stepped aside for Cal to do the same. "Come in, but be warned, you'll be interrogated by a toddler and a cockatiel."

They made it as far as the foyer when Cal was stopped by a tiny hand belonging to a little boy with Spider-Man pajama bottoms and a Wonder Woman pajama top. At least Mia thought the child was a boy.

"This is Rowen, my grandson. Once he gets his questions answered, he'll grant you entry," Megan said with an indulgent smile.

"Ah you two mahweed?" Cal looked at Mia and then Megan helplessly.

"He's asking if you two are married," Megan said as she continued to hold the rambunctious dog.

"Oh, no," Cal said. Mia felt her face flush like a teenager and mentally rolled her eyes.

"Do you like bwussel spouts?" He turned to ask Mia.

"I do," she said with a hint of triumph at deciphering the child's words.

"Bye." Off Rowen went down the hall. Megan released the dog who happily followed him, having lost interest in the newcomers too.

"How you doin'?" Mia whirled around at the high-pitched sound and saw a large cage in the corner with a cockatiel hanging upside down and swinging from a perch.

Mia furrowed her brow and answered the bird. "I'm fine, thanks."

The bird used his beak to climb back to an upright position and squawked again then started preening, effectively dismissing them.

"I'm watching Rufio and Rowen this week. My son and daughter-in-law are on babymoon number two." Megan sighed good-naturedly and gestured to the front room that already had a pile of albums on the coffee table.

They had a seat on the gray leather couch and Cal set the box of letters next to the albums. "Thank you again for agreeing to meet with us. When Cal found the letters, I couldn't help digging into your family history." Mia felt a little embarrassed at admitting that last part, but Megan didn't seem to mind one bit.

"It's actually an incredible story. My wife, Stacy, says I should write a book about it. The letters you found, they're kind of the missing piece to the puzzle. I'm so glad you reached out."

Mia smiled warmly. She was so glad she reached out too. She really looked forward to finding the answers to all their questions.

"So, the letters you found were from Anne Harris who was a pilot in the WASP? And you said the letters looked like they were never opened and that you found them in the attic of the barn? Above the apartment?" Megan asked as she brought the box to her lap and opened it. She took out the first letter, opened it gingerly and studied it in silence for a few seconds before putting it down. "You're right, the museum would love to have these. I'll make photocopies for them and send them off if that's okay?"

"Oh, well, yes. I mean, they're yours now, so..." Mia said, gesturing to the box.

Megan nodded and slipped the letter back in the envelope. "So, what did you find out about Anne?"

"She was born around here and flew her father's crop duster. That's how she got into the program. It seemed she died on a transport mission over the Colorado Rockies in 1943, though." Mia looked at Cal who had his own solemn expression at hearing Mia talk about her again.

"And Adam?" Megan asked with the barest hint of a smile.

"He came to work for the Giambi's after the war. Met Patty and they fell in love and were married. He died in..." Mia stopped, trying to remember the date but Cal was quicker.

"He died in 1976 during a fire at the winery."

Megan set the box down on the coffee table and picked up a worn leather-bound book. "Well, one of those stories is true."

Cal spoke up again. "Anne was Adam."

Mia's eyes went wide as she looked at Cal then at Megan who had a knowing smile on her lips. "That's why they... We thought... I thought they were siblings."

"Nope. Anne and Adam were one and the same." She

handed Mia the book. "This is my grandmother's writing journal. I found it buried in a trunk that held her and my grandfather's wedding outfits. She writes about everything: How her parents threatened to disown her if she kept up her 'friendship' with Anne. How upset she was when Anne went to the WASPs in Texas."

Mia turned the book over in her hands and with a nod from Megan, opened it up to a random page. She looked at Cal, whose eyes were still slightly wide with interest. She began to read aloud.

"*Tonight, over dinner, mother asked us when we were going to start trying for children. My dear, sweet 'husband' happily announced we'd been trying since our wedding night. It absolutely mortified my mother, so I think it dissuaded her from asking again for a long while.*

"*We've talked about having kids, but adoption seems like such a scary proposition. We do have an appointment at St. Paul's Episcopal Church, however, to seek guidance on how to go about starting the process. I do so wish I could carry Adam's children. To have a few of those little faces and those big, bright eyes running around? What a dream it would've been, but I wouldn't change a thing about our lives together.*"

Mia looked up at Cal, noting the wistful look in his eyes. "So, she wrote about it all? How Anne came back to her, but as Adam?" he asked.

"It's all there. There're actually two more journals just like that. I'd be happy to loan them to you one at a time. I feel like you two might really appreciate the story."

Mia's eyes grew misty as she looked at Megan then to the book in disbelief. "I can't…"

Megan leaned over and put her hand on Mia's. She smiled, then regarded Cal as well. "I want you to know their story."

"My head is still swimming. How about yours?" Mia asked as she turned onto the freeway to head back to the winery.

"Yeah..." Cal said. To have his suspicions confirmed had brought up a lot of strong emotions he hadn't anticipated. He couldn't wait to dive into Patty's diary. He had so many more questions: Was Anne an actual trans man? Or was it only a disguise to be with her love?

"I know it'll be late when we get back, but do you want to come up to the house for a while? I'd feel guilty starting to read without you, and I can guarantee you, I will be starting it tonight," Mia laughed.

"I can lose a little sleep for Patty and Adam."

They pulled into Mia's driveway a few minutes past nine and went directly to her living room where she turned on a few lights. "You want some wine or a beer or anything?"

"I think just water, please," Cal said as he took a seat on the couch.

"No starting without me," Mia called from the kitchen and Cal laughed.

"Wouldn't dream of it."

She returned with a glass of water for Cal and a glass of wine for herself. "I wish we hadn't finished that bottle of wine you made. It sure was good," Mia said as she leaned into his shoulder for a second.

"You really liked it, huh?" Cal said, quite flattered she was still thinking about it and how much she liked it. He had been intentional in bringing the wine and letting her taste it before telling her he'd been the winemaker on that vintage. He wanted her to know that losing Samuel wouldn't be as big a hardship as she thought it would be.

"I did," Mia said with a nod before she brought the glass of wine to her lips.

"What are you drinking now?" he asked.

"Oh, last year's syrah." She offered him her glass, which took him a little by surprise. He'd of course tried all the wine they produced, including that vintage, but he couldn't refuse Mia's offer to share her glass. It felt like another level of comfort between the two had been reached.

"Thanks," he said as he swirled it around a bit before taking a sip. "I think it could be improved, though." His grin was cheeky, and he knew it, but Mia took his comment in stride with her own grin.

"I think you are right." She took the glass back and set it down. "We'll get to work on it right after this year's harvest." Neither of them brought up the fact that it was Tom's last harvest that they'd be bottling in a month or so. They both seemed reluctant to dampen the mood they'd set for themselves that night.

"So, shall I start reading?" Mia asked, eyes wide with excitement as she picked up the journal and opened it to the first page.

"Yes, please," Cal said as he leaned back against the couch. Mia regarded him for a moment with an easy smile, then turned back to the book, cleared her throat and started.

July 17, 1945

I've never been one to want to write down my feelings. I'd rather just live them and get on with life. That's what I was doing after my Anne died two years ago. Even though a big part of me died alongside her, I had to keep living. I had to hide the depth of my grief so my mother and father wouldn't catch on how much she meant to me.

But today, that part of me has been revived! I still can't believe it... I think that's why I want to write this all down. In case it is a dream, at least I'll have these words to look back on.

I must also keep this diary a secret. I shouldn't even be writing this, but I have to. I have to get this all out somewhere or I'll explode! My Anne came back to me! My beautiful, brave, sweet Anne! But I must never call her that again. I must never call her, 'her' again. My Anne came back to me, but she has come back to me as Adam.

"Wow," Cal murmured as he sat back up.

"Can you imagine? After two years, she just shows up? But as a man?" Mia flipped the pages absently as she shook her head. "I wonder if Patty had a hard time loving Anne as Adam."

Cal considered the question. The dilemma of living his life the way he wanted and divulging the truth of his transition loomed large in that moment. Would it hurt less to tell her now, before his feelings grew any deeper?

"Have you ever been in love?"

The question shocked Cal out of his thoughts. He'd had a few girlfriends, but they'd all been before he'd transitioned. He'd never let them in enough to know if he could have been. "I don't think so."

She turned fully around to face him. "You've never had a..." she paused and her brow furrowed. Cal thought it was kind of cute. "Lloyd taught me never to assume..."

"I... have had girlfriends, but nothing ever serious."

"Really?" Mia regarded him with interest.

"Really. I... for a long time I never felt comfortable... in my own skin. I was also always focused on working and school..." He was getting into uncharted territory and wasn't sure what or how much he wanted to divulge.

But he was beginning to realize that regardless of the potential for more between him and Mia, he did want her to know the real him and all of his truths. But was there enough foundation to their friendship and was his heart really ready to risk it?

Mia's eyes lost their curiosity, instead growing soft, sympathetic. "Oh, Cal... You've never been in love? I mean, I wouldn't wish the heartache being in love can cause on anyone, but to feel that all-encompassing, overwhelming affection for someone? To have them be the first thing you think of in the morning and the last before you go to bed? To wonder what they are thinking all the time and to want to protect and comfort them and be their biggest champion? It's the best feeling in the world."

Cal sat back against the couch, surprised by Mia's impassioned words. It took a moment for them to sink in and when they did, his eyes widened. *Well, shit,* he thought. *I guess maybe I am in love.*

"Do you want to read a little more? Mia asked.

Cal swallowed hard. Half of him wanted to go back to his apartment so he could process his revelation. But the other half... the other half relished the excuse to stay in her company for a bit longer. "Sure."

"How about you read to me?" Mia asked as she handed the journal over with a hopeful smile.

"I'd be happy to," he said as he settled it onto his lap and turned to the next entry.

July 20, 1945

I'm so angry at my father, but I shouldn't be surprised. I learned today that Adam had written to me while he was at pilot training. I never got the letters, so I imagine my father kept them from me. He never approved of my friendship with Anne.

Adam put on a brave face when I told him I never received the letters. I know he believed me. Knowing that he hadn't heard back from me at all, letter after letter... It broke my heart. But it made it all the more special that despite that, he came back. His faith in our love is so strong. I often think to myself how do I deserve someone like him. But Adam always turns it around on me.

Maybe that's the secret to true love. Never feeling like you deserve the other person? Not that either of us is unworthy; it's the feeling of being so privileged to be loved by the other. I don't know, maybe I'm being melodramatic, but it is how I feel. Every day I wake up and feel so lucky and blessed that Adam is in my life.

"What a story, huh?" Cal said as he closed the journal, feeling himself get emotional. He tried to put himself in Anne's—Adam's shoes—trying to imagine coming back to a place that didn't accept them, risking it all to reunite with the woman they loved.

When Mia didn't answer right away, he looked over at her and saw her wiping at her eyes. "You okay?" he asked softly.

"Oh, yes. It is quite a story. What an extraordinary love they had."

"Indeed," Cal said. He wondered if Mia was thinking about Tom in that moment and was suddenly very curious about the life they shared together. He didn't know if it was appropriate to ask, however. That she loved him very much was apparent. Once again, his heart ached for her and what she had gone through.

"Well, thanks again for indulging me. It's really cool to have someone that's as interested in this as I am," Mia said as she tried to stifle a yawn.

"I appreciate you letting me come along on the journey," Cal said with a grin.

Mia's hair, which she'd worn down all day, fell forward when she nodded, obscuring her face momentarily. He started to lift his hand to tuck it behind her ear, but stopped himself. "Of course! We wouldn't even have known about had you not gone traipsing around the attic," she chuckled.

"I guess that's true." When she tried to stifle another yawn, Cal knew that was his cue to go. "I'll let you get some sleep. Thanks again for today. It was fun."

A look of disappointment flashed across her features, or maybe it was Cal's imagination. When he stood, she slowly followed. "It was fun. Hope you have a good rest, Cal. I'll see you tomorrow."

"That you will," Cal grinned. "Goodnight, Mia."

"Goodnight, Cal."

As Cal walked down the hill back to his apartment, he replayed the day he'd spent with Mia. He smiled to himself when lyrics from one of his favorite songs popped into his head. He sung them with a low mumble. "Is it really this fun when you're on my mind... Is it really this cool to be in your life..." He shook his head, letting out a self-deprecating chuckle. "I'm ridiculous."

16

Mia groaned when her alarm went off, and she leaned over to shut it off. Three o'clock in the morning came much too fast. But she couldn't stay grumpy. It was day one of the harvest and she was eager to get down to the rows and help with picking.

She got dressed and made herself a cup of coffee and a piece of toast before heading to her golf cart. The air was cool but held a hint of the warmth that was coming once the sun rose. Picking was best done at the coolest temperatures to prevent early fermentation.

"Morning." Cal greeted her enthusiastically as she pulled up next to the de-stemming and crushing machine. "Hope you got enough sleep," he said as he came over to the driver's side.

Since Mia had gotten Patty's journal a week ago, it had become a routine of sorts for Mia to call Cal after dinner and read a journal entry. They'd gotten to talking about other things though the night before and had lost track of time. "Morning, Cal. I could have used a little more, but I'll live," she replied with a rueful chuckle.

"You ready to get your harvest on?" he asked as he bounced on the balls of his feet and gave her a wide grin. His excitement was contagious, and Mia couldn't help but smile and nod. How could he have that much energy? Surely, he was up hours before her turning on the generator lights and pulling out the equipment from the barn.

"I'm ready," she said, brandishing her clippers and gloves.

They walked over to the large group of day workers as Freddie was giving them instructions in Spanish. Cal leaned over and asked Mia if she spoke Spanish. "I don't. I've been meaning to take lessons, though. You?"

"I understand it better than I can speak it." He roughly translated what Freddie was telling the workers and after a few more minutes of questions and clarifications, everyone went to their specified rows where bins were already lined up and got to work.

Cal turned to Mia, eyes bright. "Be my picking buddy? We'll take the rows we'll use for the grape stomping event. That way we only need to pick about every second or third cluster, leaving the rest to harvest the day of the event."

"Sounds good. Lead the way," Mia said with a grin.

They worked for the first half hour in companionable silence. Mia let her mind wander back to the conversation they'd had the night before regarding Patty's journal entry. It recalled how she and Adam met.

Patty had been going steady with a boy from high school at the time, and she remembered lamenting how she was sure she should be feeling something more for him. Then Patty's father had hired James Harris to dust his vineyard, and a few months into the contract, James was replaced by his daughter Anne, a bright-eyed, slight, pistol of a girl. Patty was immediately smitten but was so frightened at her feelings for another girl.

"I can't imagine how hard it would be to be gay and in high school, let alone sixty years ago," she mused aloud.

Cal, who was just opposite her on the next row, paused his cutting and looked at her for a few seconds before turning back to cutting and shrugged. "Yeah, I imagine it would be hard."

Mia regarded him for a long second. She had been around him enough now to know when he was uncomfortable. Surely, he couldn't have a problem with gay people? He got on so well with Lloyd, after all.

"Did you know anyone gay growing up?" she asked. She'd only known one gay man, Cecil, who owned the beauty salon her mom got her hair done in when she could afford it. Her town was generally unaccepting of anyone different, but they seemed to make an exception for Cecil.

He stopped cutting again and came over to her side, clipping clusters at great speed and tossing them into the adjacent bin. "I knew a few."

Again, his answer was slow in coming and short. She knew he grew up in a town similar to hers in their way of thinking. It would break her heart if after all this time, he did have a problem with gay people. But the way he was so fascinated with Patty and Anne's story... something wasn't adding up.

Cal moved back to the other row and conversation was surface and sporadic for the next couple of hours until the first tendrils of sunbeams began to crest over the foothills. "Let's take a break and watch the sunrise, huh?" Cal said as he tossed his clippers and gloves into one of the empty bins.

They walked down to the barn where Cal had a table and some coolers set out with pre-made breakfast sandwiches he'd ordered for the first day for the crew. They each grabbed one and a bottle of water and made their way over to the paddock fence. Cal set his sandwich and water on a post. He climbed up first and took Mia's from her so she could climb up too.

Once they were settled, both sat silently as sunlight bounced off the scattered clouds, filling the sky with hues of purple, pink, orange, yellow. "I love watching the sunrise," Cal said before taking a big bite of his sandwich.

"You've probably seen a lot more than I have," Mia said, enthralled with the simple beauty.

"When I was on the swim team in high school, we had practice at five thirty every morning. I did not appreciate seeing those sunrises." Cal laughed.

"I bet." Mia took another bite of her sandwich and chewed thoughtfully, their earlier conversation in the rows still on her mind. "Cal... when we were talking about gay people... You don't have a problem with them, do you?" She hadn't planned on calling him out, but the issue was too important to her not to have clarity on.

Cal swung his head around so fast, Mia was afraid he'd fall off the fence railing. "No, of course not," he said, eyes wide with indignation. "Why would you think that?"

Mia couldn't figure out if he was offended by the insinuation or being overly defensive. "You just... didn't seem like you wanted to talk about it. Like you were uncomfortable."

As she held his gaze, another thought came to her mind. Perhaps he himself was questioning? Or in deep denial? She mentally shook her head, trying to stop it from running away with suppositions.

"I guess I just don't really think about it that much. But trust me when I say, I have absolutely no problem with people being gay. At all." Cal's eyes were sincere, and his words rang true. It was a relief, but there was still something niggling in the back of her mind.

CAL SPENT THE NEXT COUPLE OF HOURS CUTTING RIGHT ALONG next to Mia but deep in thought. Even if his feelings for her only ever amounted to a solid friendship, he felt like he was lying to her by omitting such a big truth about himself. Especially in light of how Mia was reacting to Patty and Anne, or Adam's story.

Mia had given absolutely no indication that she had a problem with Patty and Anne's story. In fact, she seemed preternaturally interested in it. It gave him a slight boost of confidence that she would take his coming out in stride.

"Hey, Jefe! It's time!" Freddie called out as he appeared at the end of the row they were working on. Cal checked his watch, shocked to find that it was already eleven in the morning.

It was a tradition that at the end of the first day of harvest, all the full-time employees jumped into the pond, clothes and all before having a big barbeque to celebrate.

"Okay, okay," Mia said, waving him away as the Mule came by and picked up the bins to take to processing. "You ready to get wet?" Mia said, then immediately turned a shade of red Cal had never seen on her. It was adorable. He fought hard not to laugh outright at her unintended double entendre. Instead, he gave her a big smile and a wink.

"Beat you to the pond," he said and took off running. After a few yards, he pulled up a little to let her catch up and then overtake him. She slowed, balancing on one leg as she hopped, pulling off one boot and then the other. His cheeks hurt from the wide smile on his face as he watched her stop right before the end of the dock, whoop loudly, and jump in.

Oh, how this woman had his heart. There was no more denying it. He bent to untie his boots, letting the long-simmering truth take hold. As he slid them off and ambled toward the end of the dock, Mia stood up in the shallow part. The pale-yellow t-shirt she wore did nothing to hide the outline of her breasts and her nipples, which were stiff from the cool pond water. Cal stood, frozen in place, nearly bumped into the pond by Freddie, who raced past him and leaped into the water.

"You coming in, or what?" Mia called out to him as she smoothed her hair back from her face. He shook his head to clear it, took off at a run, and tucked into a perfect cannonball, landing a few feet from her. When he broke the surface, he was assaulted by a wave of water and a delighted laugh.

He stood, letting the water slough off him and noticed he wasn't the only one appreciating someone's physique as the water made his pale-gray shirt nearly invisible.

He wiped his face and then held out a fist. Mia grinned and bumped it with her own. "Happy harvest day, Mia."

"Happy harvest day, Cal." Mia beamed.

17

Cal trudged up the stairs to his apartment, calculating the time it would take to eat a sandwich, shower, and get into bed. It was the final day of the harvest and he'd spent the better part of the night processing the remaining bins of grapes. He was exhausted and sore, but pretty happy, overall.

He tugged off his boots the second he got inside the door and pulled off his shirt, which was stained with grape juice. He tossed it toward the bathroom as he headed to his kitchen and made himself a peanut butter and jelly sandwich and poured a glass of milk. Not even bothering to sit, he wolfed it down and then drank the milk in two big gulps.

He set the glass in the sink and walked to the bedroom where he took off his pants and set his keys and phone on the nightstand. He then went to the bathroom and turned on the shower. As he let it warm, he stripped off his underwear and socks. He caught himself in the mirror and a rush of heat came on as he thought about Mia in the pond a couple of weeks earlier.

Seeing her like that—not that he hadn't started imagining it at night when he was alone in his bed—ignited something in him that he'd not experienced, at least not at this level. He yearned to be able to touch Mia intimately.

Momentarily forgetting his exhaustion, he let his hand wander down to the copious amount of hair on his lower belly to between his thighs. He'd gone around for years about whether to get bottom surgery at all, but his dysphoria was so bad, he finally made the decision to get metoidioplasty.

He was fortunate in that he had a good amount of bottom growth on testosterone, so his surgeon was able to use his existing tissue to form a small penis. He'd decided on a vaginectomy as well as urethral lengthening so he could pee standing up. He was very happy with the results and as he healed, his dysphoria all but disappeared.

He ran his hand over himself, instantly becoming erect. He closed his eyes and stroked for a few seconds before his body reminded him how exhausted he was. He let out a wistful groan and got into the shower, making quick work of ridding himself of dirt, sweat, and grape residue, and after barely drying himself off, pulled on a pair of clean boxers and fell into bed.

Cal wasn't sure how long he'd been asleep when he was awoken by the strong smell of smoke. He sat up, taking in deep lungfuls through his nose as he tried to locate where it was coming from. The smoke alarm hadn't gone off in the apartment, so he deduced it must be coming from outside.

As he sat up and moved to the end of the bed and put his feet down, his heart dropped to his stomach. Heat radiated from the floor. The fire was in the equipment room, right under him. Leaping over the bed to the other side, he grabbed his pants and pulled them on. He ran out of his room and to the front door, taking a moment to smash his feet into his boots.

As soon as his feet hit the dirt, he ran to the front of the building where he found one of the overhead doors halfway open. He could see the orange flames licking up to the ceiling which was inches away from his floor. He ran to where the fire extinguisher was but found the space empty. "Fuck," he screamed in frustration. He ran to the outbuilding about fifty feet away and kicked the door in. He grabbed the one right by the door and ran back. He emptied it, but it did little to knock the flames down. He knew he didn't have much time before the flames got to one of the fuel tanks on one of the machines.

He stood and watched the flames for another few seconds, at a loss as to what to do. He didn't have his phone and by the looks of the flames, it may only be a matter of minutes before the whole building was engulfed. He had to make a decision. Even if he called the fire department right that second, they'd be too late.

His brain went from how to fight the fire to saving what he could. "Mia's office…" he murmured. He took off to the other side, taking the stairs two at a time until he reached the door. It took four tries, but he finally was able to kick the door in. He threw the lights on, relieved they still worked. He ran to the phone and dialed 9-1-1, punched the speaker button and reported the fire as quickly and concisely as he could.

What do I save? He looked around frantically for something to put things in. Grabbing the shredder, he knocked off the top of it and picked up the bin, dumping the already shredded documents out. He grabbed all the folders that were on Mia's desk that he figured might not have been entered in her computer yet. He then swept her photos into the bin and grabbed the picture of Mia and her husband off the wall.

Smoke was beginning to fill the room as the fire broke through the floor in the far corner of the office. He searched around for anything else he could save and saw the small wooden box that sat under Mia's monitor. He picked it up and placed that on top of everything in the bin.

He was coughing hard now, unable to breathe through the thick smoke. He crouched as low as he could and felt his way until he came to the door. He stumbled out, continuing to cough to clear his lungs. He ran to his truck, setting the bin in the bed and then went to the spigot by the outbuilding. He cranked it on and grabbed the hose, determined to do what he could before the fire department got there.

He was doing his best to keep the fire from hitting the fuel tanks when he heard the wail of fire truck sirens and then their flashing lights coming down the hill. He jogged out of the way as they quickly got to work knocking down the flames.

His hands went to his knees, and he let go of the hose as he was overcome by a coughing fit. "Cal!" He looked up and saw Mia running toward him in men's pajamas and a robe, barefoot. He was barely able to stand upright before she crashed into him, holding him tight against her for what felt like a full minute.

She finally released him and before he could speak, she grabbed his face and brought him down for a short, but forceful kiss. His eyes didn't even have time to close before her lips retreated from his. "When I heard the sirens and saw... I thought you were..."

Her hands remained on either side of his face, holding and staring at him with wide, glistening eyes. He didn't even think she realized she kissed him. "I'm okay. I was able to save some stuff from your office..." He trailed off as he looked up toward his apartment. Whatever the fire wasn't destroying, the water from the fire hoses was saturating. Everything was replaceable though, and he could retrieve the fire safe with all of his important documents once the fire was out.

He wasn't sure if she heard him as she stepped back to inspect him. It was then he remembered he'd not thought to pull on a shirt. But between his chest hair, the soot coating his skin and the darkness, he doubted she could see his scars.

"Are you sure you're okay?" she asked as she continued to look him over.

"You need paramedics, sir?" one of the firefighters asked as she approached them.

"Oh, no. I'm okay," he said, stifling a cough as best he could. He caught eyes with Mia who regarded him skeptically. "I'm fine. Inhaled a bit of smoke is all."

The fire was almost out when another car came driving down the hill. The firefighter who offered to call the ambulance gestured to the man getting out of it as she held out a thin blanket. "That's Captain Followill. He's going to ask you some questions about what happened."

Cal wrapped the blanket around his shoulders, suddenly feeling very exposed. It stung and he wondered if he wasn't a little singed.

"Hello, I'm Captain Jim Followill," the man said as he brandished a small notebook and pen. "What happened here tonight?"

Cal relayed the whole thing to him and Mia and when

he was done, the captain shut his notebook. "Thank you. We'll be here for a while, trying to figure out how this started. You have a place to stay in the meantime?"

Mia spoke up. "Yes, he does. He'll be up at the house with me."

Cal looked at her with mild surprise. He hadn't even thought about what he was going to do. But it was sinking in now. The only things he had now were what he had on his body. He had no idea what had survived. "Thanks, Mia."

They stayed talking to Captain Followill for another half an hour, answering all of his questions to the best of their ability. Cal had no idea how the fire started, but he knew he'd shut and locked both overhead doors before heading up to his apartment.

The short ride to Mia's house was quiet. Cal was fighting to stay awake, the adrenaline wearing off some time ago. He could feel Mia's eyes on him every few seconds and he wondered if she was thinking about that kiss she'd given him. His mind kept coming back to it, even after all that had happened that night.

Mia pulled right up to the side door by the kitchen and Cal slid out of the seat and went to the back of the cart to grab the bin of stuff from her office. Mia waved him off. "I've got it. Door's unlocked, go ahead and go in."

Her tone brooked no argument and he nodded and walked to the door, opening it and holding it ajar for Mia. "Thanks for putting me up," he said again. The cool air in the house made him shiver as Mia set the bin down on the kitchen table.

"It's the least I could do." She reached into the bin and pulled out the wooden box. Her hand went to her mouth and Cal could see the glisten of unshed tears in the low light. She set the box down reverently and studied Cal. "I can't believe you did that... went to my office instead of your apartment." Her eyes searched his as the weight of his actions settled between them.

"Mia... I have something I need to tell you." He couldn't wait another second. This was either going to set him free or crush him, but he had to tell her before anything else was said between them.

"I'm trans. I'm a trans man."

Mia's eyes blinked rapidly in confusion, then grew wide in surprise. "You're transgender?"

"Yes. I was assigned female at birth—"

"I know what transgender means," Mia interrupted softly as her hands slipped off Cal and settled at her sides.

Cal's heart was pounding so hard it hurt. A precursor of what was to come, he was sure. "I'm sorry I didn't tell you sooner..."

Mia's eyes shot up to Cal's. "Hey, it's okay. You don't owe me any explanation."

"Okay," Cal managed. God, he really felt exposed now, and not just physically. Mia seemed to have read his mind.

"Let's get you some clean clothes. Then we can talk."

Cal nodded and followed Mia as she started toward the bedrooms. Cal stopped in the hallway, but Mia didn't go to her bedroom, she went to the guest room. Cal heard the sound of a few drawers opening and closing and then Mia reappeared with a t-shirt and some sweatpants.

"I hope these will do. Sweats might be a little long. You want to shower first?"

"Yes, that would be good, thank you." Cal turned to walk to the guest bathroom but a hand placed gently on his back stopped him.

"It looks like you were burned, Cal," Mia said as she

traced around a spot on his left shoulder. "I'll put some aloe on it after your shower, okay?"

He tried not to shiver at her ghost of a touch. "Yes, thank you," he said in a hoarse whisper that had as much to do with her soft fingers against his skin as it did his raw throat.

18

Mia sat at the kitchen table, waiting for Cal to get out of the shower. She idly spun the bottle of aloe around, deep in thought. She was so overcome with gratitude that Cal had saved something so precious to her. Her mother's nursing pin that she'd sacrificed so much for. She was so happy and proud to be a nurse, even if it was only for a short while before she got sick. Mia had been so proud of her too.

And the photos. He'd even thought to grab the one off the wall. That consideration for her, putting her things before his. She knew she was falling for him now. There was no question.

The news that Cal was trans had surprised her, but only because she'd never considered that he might be. Looking back on the perceived discomfort about gay people, him being adamant about not letting her go into the hospital with him, it made sense now.

She heard the door to the bathroom open and called out to Cal to let him know where she was. A few moments later, he was joining her in the dining room. He had on the sweats and the clean pair of socks, holding the t-shirt in his hands. "Uh, I waited to put the shirt on..." He gestured to his shoulder and Mia smiled.

A surge of emotion welled up, along with a hint of arousal. It took her by surprise, and she pushed it aside. "Have a seat," she said as she got up and poured a bit of the aloe gel in her hand. "Lean forward a little?"

He complied and Mia scooped up most of it onto her fingers and checked to make sure there were no other angry, red areas. Then she began to gently rub the gel onto the spot on his shoulder. He jerked upright and Mia pulled her fingers away in alarm.

"Sorry, it's just cold after the warm shower," he said with a shiver. She smiled, continuing to rub the gel in as her eyes moved over his defined back muscles. His skin was smooth, not much hair. She noticed the hair on the back of his neck was getting kind of long. He was overdue for a haircut, she thought.

"There. Let it dry for a minute and you can put your shirt on," Mia said as she capped the bottle. "Do you want something to drink?"

"Oh, yeah, water would be great. My throat is still a little sore." He brought his hand up to his throat and rubbed it absently.

She poured herself a glass of water as well, bringing them to the table and then sitting back down. "Thanks for patching me up once again."

"Yeah, I thought I told you to stop getting hurt on my vineyard." Her voice was light, belying the visceral fear she'd experienced an hour ago.

Cal gave her a half-smile and nodded before he grew serious. "So, you want to talk about... what I told you?"

"Only if you are up to it. I know you must be exhausted."

Mia looked down at her water glass, trying to order her thoughts. She was worried about how much damage was done to the barn, how much they'd lost, but she knew she had to let the fire department finish their work before she could get down there and see.

But this thing with Cal, it had been building for months, and with the news that he was transgender, there was a lot for them to talk about.

"I'd rather just get it over with," he said, prompting Mia's eyes to catch his in a gentle regard. He looked down at his water glass and shook his head slowly before looking back up. "Sorry. I've tried this one other time, and it did not go well."

Mia gave him a sympathetic smile. She imagined it would be so hard to have to be so vulnerable so early in a relationship and then be rejected for it. *Relationship?* Mia mentally shook her head at the premature thought. "I'll admit, I'm surprised, but that's not..." Mia closed her eyes for a second, knowing she needed to be careful with her words. When she opened them, Cal was regarding her with an open expression. It gave her the courage to not only voice what had been building, unspoken, between them, but to be completely honest with him. "It isn't a big deal to me, Cal. I like you. A lot."

"You like me, huh? A lot?" His smile was edging toward amusement and Mia realized she might have overplayed her hand. *Damnit, Lloyd, were you wrong? Shit, maybe he doesn't feel the same.*

Before she could sink into her chair in embarrassment, Cal reached out and covered her hand with his own. "Hey, I like you too. A lot. It's why I told you about me." He straightened up in his chair, pulling her hand slightly as his eyes narrowed. "You are the strongest, kindest, most interesting woman I've ever met."

"Not the prettiest?" Mia teased as she fluttered her eyelashes.

"If I had a dollar for every time I caught myself staring at you, I'd have enough to buy my own vineyard," Cal said with an earnest smile.

"Well, you're pretty easy on the eyes too, I guess," Mia said with a playful.

"Really?" Cal asked.

The genuine disbelief in his voice made Mia's heart drop. She put her other hand over his. "I think you are incredibly handsome. It was one of the first things I mentioned to Lloyd when I told him I'd hired you," Mia said, feeling herself blush at the admission. But she wanted Cal to know the truth.

"So, you hired me for my looks, then?" Cal's smirk held a hint of genuine delight and that made Mia's heart do a low swoop through her chest.

"They didn't hurt." She winked.

Cal's smirk turned into a sheepish grin. "I can't believe we had this conversation with me shirtless."

Mia's eyes unconsciously traveled to his chest, where she saw the faint, small scars under his lower pectoral muscles.

He scooted his chair out and leaned back slightly and traced a scar with his finger. "Luckily, I wasn't very endowed. Not much to take out." Mia's eyes snapped up to his, contrite. "It's okay. I'll admit, I'm not out to many people who didn't know me before my transition. Well, hardly anyone. You and Dr. Sage."

Mia's jaw fell open slightly. Dr. Sage was the doctor she'd recommended when Cal broke his arm. "That's it?"

He nodded. "Yes. I wanted..." He stopped, took a breath, and started again. "I want to live my life on my terms. It's why I moved. I want to be the one in control of who I tell and when..." He looked down at his chest and then back up again. "I'm not ashamed that I'm trans. Not at all. The fact that I lived the first twenty-five years of my life presenting female has given me a perspective that no cis man has, you know?"

It was strange, hearing Cal refer to his life as a woman. No wonder he was so fascinated with Adam's story. "It must have been hard, living where you did and having to transition there, huh?"

"I was supported at home. My dad and my sister were great. My mom had a hard time at first, but she came around. They helped me through my surgeries and put up with me when I was adjusting to the testosterone." He smiled wistfully before his lips gave way to a pinched frown. "That's about as far as my support went. People are not open-minded where I grew up. They'd intentionally misgender me, well after I'd transitioned, just to be hateful. It wore me down."

"I'm sorry," Mia said, realizing their hands were still intertwined. "Well, for what it's worth, I'm so very glad you landed here." She gave him a warm smile, which he returned.

"I am too. So much so."

They fell silent for a moment, holding each other's gaze. Though she wanted to talk to Cal more, Mia could see the exhaustion in his eyes. "Why don't you go get some sleep. I'll head down to the barn to see how things are going."

She'd consciously kept Samuel's name out of her mouth, as did Cal when talking to the fire captain. But she knew Cal would have absolutely locked the overhead doors. Samuel could have easily had a key made when he was in possession of them. She wanted to wait until they determined the cause of the fire though, before bringing up his name.

"I could go with you," Cal said but his last word was lost in a poorly stifled yawn.

Mia patted his hand. "Nah, I'm going to need you rested for when it's time to clean up," she said with a grim smile.

She winced at her words when Cal sighed heavily. "Yeah, I wonder if any of my stuff survived... my guitar..." He sat up, shaking his head. "No, I'm not gonna think about it... Everything is replaceable..."

She knew he was putting on a brave face for her. She couldn't imagine having to wonder if everything she owned was destroyed. "I know it is of little solace, but insurance should cover everything lost. And if it doesn't cover something, I will. Also, did I mention how much I love clothes shopping?"

That got an amused smile out of him. "Good, because I hate it," he said as he stood and pulled his shirt on. Mia only hesitated a second before she rose out of her chair and moved to stand in front of him.

With deliberate slowness, she reached up and cupped his jaw. When he smiled and slipped his hand over hers, she pressed forward, rising up on her toes. "I'm going to kiss you now," she whispered, poised to stop if Cal gave any indication he did not want that. He bent his head to close the distance.

Mia closed her eyes, lost in the soft warmth of Cal's lips and the gentle tickle of his mustache. She let out something between a sigh and a moan when Cal pressed closer. The hand that had been covering hers against his cheek moved to her lower back and pulled her in slowly.

She hadn't thought, only acted, much like she did that first frantic kiss when she saw Cal was okay. She expected the kiss to feel right, and it did—but she knew the timing was not. Slowly, she pulled away. She smiled when Cal's eyes remained closed. She had lowered her heels and removed her hand from his jaw before he finally opened them. He gave her a radiant smile. "That was... unexpected. And really, really nice."

She returned his smile for a moment before it faltered. "Listen, I'm not sure I'm ready for anything more... at least right now..." She dropped her head and bit her lip for a second before looking back up. "I shouldn't have kissed you..."

"Again." Cal's smile had become smaller, but it was still there. The corner of Mia's lips twitched in acknowledgment. He didn't seem fazed at her admission, and she took it as a good sign. A really good sign.

"Look, I know you've been through so much the last couple of years. I respect that and I respect you. I just want you to know, I'm not going anywhere. Not unless you want me to, okay?"

She could do it... She could throw herself into his arms right now and ask him to help her forget all of her pain and grief, but that wouldn't be fair to him, and it wouldn't help her in the long run. She could almost see a future with Cal, but she had to be sure she was ready to cultivate that into a fruitful reality.

She nodded, not trusting her voice.

19

Cal woke to a low buzzing sound and slowly opened his eyes. He looked around, immediately confused. *Oh, right. The fire. I'm in Mia's guest room.* The events of the night before, or rather, earlier that morning played through his mind. His throat was a little sore, but overall he felt okay. He was anxious and afraid to go down to the barn to see what was left of it. What was left of his possessions.

Then he remembered what happened after the fire. He couldn't believe he'd finally come out to Mia, and she hadn't rejected him or accused him of being deceitful. She'd taken it in stride and had even admitted she liked him. *A lot.*

He couldn't help but smile. Especially when he recalled the kiss. Well, both of them... but that second one... Cal took Mia at her word when she said she wasn't ready for anything more, but that kiss—it held promise.

He slipped out of bed and pulled the borrowed sweats and t-shirt on, noting he barely felt the burn on his shoulder. He sure hoped some of his clothes had survived. His boxers were going on two days, and he was sure they smelled of sweat and smoke.

He opened the bedroom door and was hit with the scent of freshly ground coffee and eggs, and his stomach rumbled audibly. The peanut butter and jelly sandwich he had hours ago had barely put a dent in his hunger. He wondered what time it was.

"Morning, or should I say, afternoon," Mia said, turning around from her spot at the stove with a warm smile. "Coffee is brewing, and I made you some eggs. Took a guess and made scrambled," she said as she plated eggs and a couple of pieces of toast for herself and Cal.

"Thank you. You're very kind to feed me. I'd probably eat them raw at this point. What time is it?" he asked as squinted at the microwave clock.

"It's the least I could do," Mia said. "It's twelve thirty."

"Oh wow. You could have woken me up," he said as he buttered his toast. He watched as Mia put cream and sugar into his coffee in the ratio he liked and got a flash of an idyllic future where breakfast together was a common occurrence. He tempered his wistful smile as she came to join him, sitting next to him at the breakfast bar.

"You obviously needed the sleep. I called Freddie, and he's got the crew going through the equipment room and pulling everything out. The damage was somewhat extensive, but the structure is still sound. The captain commended you for what you did to keep the fire from the tanks. He said that was the difference."

Cal gave a sad smile, acknowledging Mia's words. He was pretty sure the barn would just be a pile of ashes if those tanks caught. "Can we go up to the second floor now?" Cal asked.

"They concluded the investigation a couple of hours ago,

so we can... I already took a look at your apartment. There's a lot of water damage, but it looked like the fire stayed mostly on the first floor."

Cal nodded. He would remain hopeful until he could get up there. The news of the investigation being concluded was surprising though. "That was fast. They determined a cause, then?"

"Arson."

Cal nodded, not surprised. "You told Followill about Samuel?"

Mia's eyes hardened in anger. "I sure did. Told him everything."

Cal shook his head. *The fucking bastard.* "I should have been more aware... probably should have gone to the police when he threatened—"

Mia interrupted him, squeezing his arm gently. "This isn't on you. I should have been the one to report him. And you locked those doors. That asshole broke into them. If it wasn't for you, the barn and who knows what else would be gone." Mia's eyes were glassy as she shook her head slowly. "If you hadn't smelled the smoke early, Cal..." She set down her fork and wiped at her eyes.

Cal turned to her and put a hand over hers. "Hey, I did though. Your office is mostly okay, right?"

"I don't care about that, you dummy," she said, chuckling incredulously through her tears. "I mean, I do care, but I was talking about you."

"Oh, right." Cal gave her a sheepish smile and then frowned. "So glad history didn't repeat itself."

Mia looked at him, stricken, and Cal could have kicked himself. "I—I meant Adam... and the fire..." God, he felt about an inch tall. Of all the insensitive things he could have said... "Shit, Mia, I'm sorry," he said, eyes pleading for forgiveness.

Mia's eyes focused on her plate as Cal studied her, wondering what else he could do or say to let her know how sorry he was for saying what he did.

After a few seconds, she looked up at him, and Cal could see the effort it took for her to smile, trying to comfort him. "It's okay, Cal. Really. I know you didn't mean... I knew you meant the fire from before."

He didn't want to keep on about it, so he nodded, letting out a breath. Mia put a hand on his knee as her face took on an earnest expression. "I don't go around hugging and kissing people for no reason, Cal. I was pretty damn relieved history didn't repeat itself too."

He fought a smile at Mia's attempt at levity. She was purposely making herself vulnerable to put him at ease. How could he not fall for this woman even more? "Outside of my family, I've never had someone as concerned for my wellbeing as you are."

Mia straightened in her chair as her eyes went a little wide at his admission. It was his turn to drop his head in embarrassment. There was a fingertip under his jaw a few seconds later, and he looked up into warm, amber eyes. "I'm sad I'm the first, but honored."

Cal pulled in a shuddering breath as he felt his eyes well up. "Damn..." He rubbed at them with the heel of his hand as he tried to get a grip. *Must be the residual emotions from last night.*

"Hey, no matter what we become to each other, I can safely say, I'll always care about what happens to you." Cal wondered if it would be a good time to lean over and kiss her, but the moment passed quickly as Mia playfully slapped his knee. "Now finish breakfast. You need your strength to help with the barn clean up."

"Oh, that's why you fed me." Cal chuckled, exceptionally happy for a man who might have lost the bulk of his worldly possessions.

Mia gave him a sly smile as she raised a hand to his face and brushed something out of his beard. "You found me out."

"Want me to go up with you or do you want to do it on your own?" Mia asked. They'd surveyed what Freddie had pulled out of the equipment room and had made a list of what needed repairs and what needed replacing. They then went up into Mia's office and went over a plan to get everything moved out so they could have a construction and restoration team come in.

Mia knew Cal had been reluctant to go into his apartment, despite his concern about his stuff. She offered to give him space if he needed it, but also wanted to be there for him for support.

"You can come up if you'd like," he said as he eyed the wide-open door at the top of the stairs.

"I'd like to." She smiled, waiting a second for him to start up the stairs, but when he didn't, she put a hand on his shoulder.

"You okay?" she asked.

He opened his eyes wide for a flash, steeling himself. "Yeah. I mean, everything is replaceable. I'm sure my fire safe is intact." He took a deep breath and let it out in a rush. "Let's do this."

She followed him up the stairs and held herself back for

a moment as he walked in. They had brought flashlights as the power had been shut off until they could make all the wall repairs. Cal went right to the blinds in the living room and opened them up, bathing the area in light.

"Ah, man." Cal's guitar was laying on the floor, adjacent to where the fire had breached the floor joists. It was obvious that it had been dowsed with water.

"I'm sorry, Cal. I didn't see it when I came through here..." She doubted there was anything she could have done to save it, but still she felt bad.

"That's okay." His voice was so sad, and Mia just wanted to give him a hug. He picked it up, turned it upside down, and grimaced as some water poured out of the sound hole. He set it against the wall gently and stepped back. "It was a graduation gift from my mom. I should have grabbed it..."

Mia approached Cal slowly with her arms out and he gave her a sad smile as he closed the distance. She wrapped her arms around him and pressed her face into his shoulder. "I'm so sorry Cal. No way to fix it?"

He shook his head. "No. Spruce and water don't mix." She leaned back, looking at him with a furrowed brow. He gave her a rueful smile. "The guitar is made out of spruce. Not water resistant at all." He slowly pulled out of their embrace and bowed his head. "Thank you... we can keep going."

They spent about an hour going through the apartment and with the exception of most of his books and photos he'd had on the bookshelf in the living room, everything else of his was salvageable. Since the apartment had come furnished, it would be easy just to replace what needed replacing once all the repairs were done.

They used the trash bags under the sink to put all of Cal's clothes and shoes in. Mia took all the clothes from the closet as he went into the bathroom. He came out with his toiletry bag and another smaller bag. "Looks like my vials of testosterone made it through," he said as he took one out and shook it. "The bathroom was relatively untouched, luckily."

"That's some good news." She smiled as she continued taking items off hangers and stuffing them into bags. They would all need to go to the dry cleaners anyway to get the smoke out of them. In the back of the closet, she pulled out a charcoal suit and laid it on the bed. "This is a nice suit." She ran her finger under the lapel, admiring the quality craftsmanship.

"Thanks. Spent a pretty penny on that. My dad said a man should own at least one nice suit."

"Well, someday, I hope to see you in it," she said, too shy to look up. She hadn't meant to say that out loud.

"I hope someday I'll have an occasion to wear it, then," he said softly.

Just then, a soft chime rang out. "Oh, my phone," Cal said and walked to the kitchen. He walked back into the bedroom as he answered it. "Yes, this is Cal. Hello, Captain Followill… Really? Okay, that's good… Yes, I'll be available to come down anytime they need… Yes, Mrs. Torwood as well. Thanks for the call."

"What was that about?" Mia asked.

"Police picked up Samuel for questioning, and apparently, they already have enough to hold him. Captain Followill just wanted to give us a heads up as we might be called down to the station."

Mia sat down on the bed and let out a relieved sigh. She hadn't realized how anxious she was about Samuel being free to roam around until that very moment. "Thank goodness."

"I still can't believe he tried to burn down the barn." Cal shook his head as he finished putting the rest of his toiletries in a bag. "You know, I almost came out to you earlier... when Samuel was starting to give you trouble. I had my fair share of sexist, misogynistic assholes I had to deal with before I transitioned."

Mia regarded him, allowing herself a second to try to imagine Cal as someone other than Cal.

"You're trying to picture what I looked like as a woman," Cal said, biting off an amused smile.

Mia winced, surprised how easy he read her. She grinned guiltily.

"It's okay to be curious. It's also okay to ask me any questions. Honestly. I'm an open book to those I trust."

Mia was touched. "Yeah?"

"Absolutely."

Mia couldn't think of any questions to ask at that moment, but she figured she would at some point in the future. The future—Mia found herself quite looking forward to future things with Cal. The thought scared and thrilled her at the same time.

"For what it's worth, I appreciate you helping me with Samuel, yet still respecting my position as owner. Though I could have handled the whole situation better..."

Cal shook his head. "No one could have predicted the guy was crazy enough to try to actually burn down the barn. Lesson learned, right?"

"Right." Mia wondered if it was the barn he was trying to destroy... or Cal. The thought chilled her to the bone. "Well, one thing is for sure, I'm getting cameras installed down here and at the production building."

"I think that is a great idea."

"Well, roommate, you got everything?" Mia said with a grin, wanting to lighten the mood.

"Roommate?" Cal said, eyebrows hiking up to his forehead.

"Well, if you want to stay in the guest room while we get the repairs done..." She trailed off, feeling unsure all of a sudden. Was it wise to have Cal in such close proximity?

"I can get a hotel room close by," Cal said, eyebrows coming back down to show concern.

Mia mentally shook her head. She could handle having him close. She actually wanted him there. Especially if they had to release Samuel for whatever reason.

"If you are okay with staying at the house, I'd like you to," she said, feeling much more confident about her offer.

"You sure?" The light in his eyes bolstered her confidence.

"I'm absolutely sure."

"All right then, roommate." Cal beamed and Mia couldn't help but beam back at him.

PART 6: CRUSH

20

"Well, hello, handsome!" Lloyd exclaimed after Cal leaned over and pushed the passenger seat door to his truck open. He shook his head as Lloyd tossed his suitcase into the backseat and climbed in next to him. "Let me guess, Mia is freaking out about tomorrow and sent you because she's too busy... freaking out."

"Kinda. Though the freak out is a bit warranted. The band that was supposed to be opening the festival tomorrow had to cancel. Three out of the four have food poisoning," Cal said with a shrug.

"Oh damn. I guess no one is available on twelve hours notice, huh?"

"We'll find out once we get back. She's been on the phone pretty much all day."

Cal had thought of offering to fill in—he knew enough cover songs to play for a couple of hours—but without his guitar, it was pretty pointless.

"Well, I can dust off my high school DJ skills," Lloyd said as he blew on his nails and polished them on his shirt.

"We just might have to resort to that."

Lloyd clapped excitedly. "I'll build a playlist tonight!"

Cal laughed. "So, how's San Fran?"

"Fucking busy as hell. I swear, the tourists are getting more entitled and ruder every season." He rolled his eyes and shook his head. "Anyway, what about you? Mia told me all about the fire and that piece of shit who set it. He's still in jail, right?"

"Yep. No one's coming to help him with bail, so he has to stay until his trial."

"Well, thank sweet Jesus for that. Mia told me about your heroics too, saving stuff from her office and her mom's nursing pin."

Cal felt his cheeks grow warm at the mention of Mia talking about him. "Yeah, I thought the files that were sitting on top of her desk were more important than my *Kill Bill* poster and four pairs of jeans."

"What you did for Mia, that's beyond selfless, Cal. You really care for her, don't you?"

It was more a statement than a question and it gave him the impression Mia had told him about the shift in their friendship. Once again, he wished for someone to be close to like that. Someone he could talk to about Mia. He supposed he could talk to his sister, but as supportive as she was, he doubted she would think falling for his boss, let alone dating her, would be a good idea.

"Yeah, I do," Cal confirmed.

He felt Lloyd's eyes on him for a few seconds before he clapped Cal on the shoulder. "So, gonna be a full house at Casa de Mia, huh? You took the bedroom closest to the bathroom, didn't you?" he said with his eyes narrowed.

"Hey, it's the room she gave me..." Cal said with a chuckle. "I can switch if you'd prefer that one."

Lloyd waved a hand dismissively. "Nah, the other one gets cooler, so…" Cal looked over at him and then shook his head. "Or we could just share…" Lloyd said, fluttering his eyelashes, eliciting a bark of laughter from Cal. "Could you imagine telling Mia when we get to the house?" Lloyd cackled, thoroughly amused with himself. "What a funny prank that would be!"

Cal had never been a prankster. He tried to imagine Mia's reaction. Did Lloyd prank Mia a lot? Did Mia pull pranks? That was definitely a side to her he'd yet to see. He hoped he would get the chance to find out all the different sides of her.

"Anyway…" Lloyd drew out as he settled back in his seat. "How are things going?"

Cal was sure Lloyd left the question vague on purpose. He knew Mia talked to Lloyd about everything, but he was hesitant to go into any sort of detail about his own feelings. "Things are slowly getting back to normal. We've got all the equipment repaired and replaced. The contractor is busy repairing the barn. Should be done in about a month."

Lloyd nodded. "I know Mia puts on a brave face, but how is she really doing?"

Cal considered the question. They'd both been so busy. He with the equipment and post-harvest tasks, and Mia with getting her new office set up in a small area next to the tasting room. She'd also been focused on planning the grape crushing event, which meant they'd barely had time to talk.

"I think she's holding up well. Definitely keeping busy, as you can imagine."

"Yeah. It's the main reason I came down. I wanted to help her out with this shindig. I wish I could have come down earlier, but owning your own restaurant makes it near impossible to get away for any length of time."

"Well, I do know she's beyond happy and grateful you are here."

Lloyd gave Cal a cheeky smile. "Oh, I know she is."

When Mia heard the rumble of Cal's truck, she set down the white tablecloth and walked out to the driveway. She waved as they parked and Lloyd jumped out and jogged over to greet her.

"Hey, hon. So happy to see you." He rumbled into her ear as he squeezed her hard in a big bear hug. "I'm so sorry about what happened and that I couldn't come down sooner."

"Well, you are here now, and I couldn't be more glad. Especially with how much work I still need to do for tomorrow," she said with a weary chuckle.

"You've got me too." Cal walked up, waving his hand.

An overwhelming sensation of contentment rolled over Mia as she looked his way. Since Cal's confession—as well as hers—she'd been putting in a lot of work, both mentally and emotionally, trying to gauge whether she was ready for a new chapter in her life that could include Cal.

She'd been reading over Patty's journal entries again, surprised at how helpful she found them. Reading their love story, their daily struggles and triumphs. In a few ways, it was like a little window into the future she and Cal might have if she had the courage to face her fears and follow her heart where she knew it wanted to lead.

"Excellent." She smiled at Cal and then turned to Lloyd. "You want to get settled in first?"

"Nah, I'm good. Put me to work."

"Okay, then. Can you two roll out the tubs for the grape stomping competition and put them on the platforms?"

Both men nodded and got to work while Mia continued laying out the tablecloths on the round tables set up around the grassy area. They worked until well after the sun had set and finished under the warm glow of the string lights.

"You know, Mia, this would be a cool area to host weddings. It's the perfect size, and you already have a lot of the set up you'd need," Lloyd said as he waved his hand over the tables and the white tent Mia had bought to house the outdoor tasting bar for the event.

Mia put her hands on her hips and looked around. She had given it a fleeting thought after she'd revamped the outdoor area, but now that Lloyd had mentioned it—he had an excellent eye for stuff like that—she knew she should seriously consider it.

"It would certainly be another great revenue stream," Cal said as he came to stand next to Mia.

"Also, a lot of work," Mia countered.

"You can hire temp workers until you establish a set calendar," Lloyd said. He then snapped his fingers and made a show of looking around again. "You know what you could also use? A restaurant that handles the catering side."

Mia turned to look at him. "Why in the world would I want to get into the restaurant..." Her words died off as his face split into a wide grin. "You want to expand? Down here? On my vineyard?" She felt her own lips stretch into a wondrous grin.

"I've been thinking about it since you moved down here. I want to hire someone to help manage Feast anyway. Plus, it would be cool to be able to write off coming down as a business expense."

"I'd love that," Mia said as she walked over and gave him an exuberant hug.

"My cooking woes would be over for sure," Cal said with a laugh.

Mia released Lloyd and laughed at Cal. "Of course, that would be the first thing you'd think of."

He let out a self-deprecating chuckle. "Guess you're getting to know me pretty well."

Mia gazed at him for a moment, thoughtful. "I guess I am."

"Wow, Lloyd, thank you. That was delicious." Cal leaned back and patted his stomach. Even after working for hours getting everything set up for the next day, Lloyd still managed to fix them a wonderful vegetable stir-fry for a late-night dinner just from what Mia had in her fridge.

"Thank you, and you are welcome." Lloyd smiled as he stood to collect the dishes.

"I'll help with those," Cal said as he stood quickly and grabbed Mia's dishes as well.

"Well, such service." Mia laughed in delight. She then groaned in frustration. "I've got a few more frantic phone calls to make to try to find an opening band for tomorrow." Lloyd raised his hand and opened his mouth, but Mia cut him off with an appreciative smile. "As much as I'm sure your DJ skills are unmatched, Lloyd, I'd like to have live music. It's classier," she said with a wink.

"Well, aside from being deeply offended, I was going to suggest that Cal play." Lloyd huffed.

"I lost my guitar in the fire. Well, it was damaged by the water."

Lloyd's face fell and Cal gave him a sad smile but then narrowed his eyes. "How did you know I played?"

Lloyd pointed to Mia. "She says you're pretty good, too."

Cal looked at Mia, who had a sheepish smile on her face. "The wall between your apartment and my office is pretty thin." Cal wasn't mad in the least. On the contrary, he was flattered that Mia had thought to even mention it to Lloyd.

"I mean, if you need me to play, I'd be happy to. I'd just need to find a guitar, I guess." Cal's mind began working, thinking about where he could go to get a guitar last minute.

"I could possibly help you out with that," Mia said, her smile still holding a shyness to it. She stood from the table and held up a finger. "I'll be right back."

Cal looked at Lloyd in confusion, but Lloyd just shrugged. Cal hurried to the kitchen, carrying the dishes and putting them in the sink. By the time he got back to the dining room, Mia had returned, holding a guitar case.

"I... uh, looked up the kind of guitar you had. I was going to surprise you with it after the festival..." Her voice died off as she placed the case gently on the table.

"Mia..." Cal whispered. He couldn't believe she'd gone out and got him the same guitar. It wasn't the most expensive one out there, but it was pricey. "You didn't have to do that," he said, even as he moved to the case, running his fingers over it before finding the latches and popping them open. He lifted the lid and stared at the instrument. Sure enough, it was the same kind, color and all.

"I hope it's okay that I did, though. I know your mother got it for you—"

Mia was unable to finish her sentence because Cal had wrapped her into a tight embrace. He held her so tight her face had been pressed to his shoulder. Her arms came up around his back after a beat and she held him just as tight.

"Thank you, so much," Cal said, fighting not to feel too overwhelmed. It was hard.

"You're welcome, Cal. I hope you don't think it too self-serving that I gave it to you now..." she said with a light chuckle.

"It's totally fine, and I'd be happy to play if you want. I know that would be one less thing you'd have to worry about."

"It would. And I'd love to hear you play," Mia said with a warm, affectionate smile.

"Then it's settled. Any requests? I probably need to go sequester myself in my room and practice," Cal said as he looked back down at the guitar. He was looking forward to getting it tuned and seeing how it sounded.

"I'll have to think about it," Mia said.

"Can I still make my playlist? I've got some real bangers on there. Maybe I can DJ the after party," Lloyd said as he pulled out his phone and cued up a Nicki Minaj song and played it at full volume.

Mia reached over and snatched the phone from his hand, turned it down and handed it back. "You are too much sometimes, my friend."

21

Cal dumped the last of the grapes into the tub and stood to stretch his back.

"You better get going. I'll bring it back to the barn," Lloyd said as he reached for Cal's empty container. They had spent the morning filling the tubs with the grapes that would be used for the grape stomping competitions while Mia directed all the vendors where to set up.

"Thanks," Cal said. He wouldn't say he was necessarily nervous to perform in front of a crowd. He'd only ever played in front of friends and family, but he reasoned that he would just be background music, and no one would be paying much attention to him as the festival got underway.

Cal ran up to the house and went to the guest room he was still staying in. He pulled out a pair of dark jeans and a short-sleeved cranberry-colored button down. He was so relieved a majority of his clothes just needed a thorough washing to get the smoke smell out.

With his outfit picked out, he headed to the bathroom to take a quick shower. He toweled off, put deodorant on, and combed his hair. He muttered to himself when he realized he'd forgotten to bring clean clothes to the bathroom with him.

No one's in the house anyway and it's just across the hall, he reasoned as he wrapped the towel around himself and grabbed his dirty clothes in one hand. He made it one step before he heard a quiet, 'Oh' and looked up to see Mia standing stock-still at the beginning of the hallway.

"Sorry, hi, I was just grabbing some extra towels for clean up..." Mia gestured to the cabinet at the end of the hall, eyes wide as she took in Cal's form.

"No problem. I forgot to bring clean clothes with me." He shrugged, kind of enjoying how flustered Mia was.

"Well, don't let me kis—keep you..." she amended quickly as her cheeks turned pink. "I'll just get the towels." She finished and rushed by Cal, not even giving him a chance to cross to his room first.

He continued to stand there as Mia pulled out a pile of towels that had definitely seen better days. He tried not to smirk, but she was just so cute and flustered. He was thoroughly reveling in the affect his near-nakedness had on her. It was such new territory for him.

"I'll see you out there, Mia," he said. For an instant, he wondered how she would react if he winked. He couldn't bring himself to do it though, settling for a crooked grin.

"I look forward to seeing you play," she said, stopping between him and the guest room door.

His smile grew. "I doubt you'll have a chance to even hear me. You're gonna be pretty busy."

"I'll make time," she said quietly and before Cal could respond, she stepped around him and headed out the back door.

The festival was underway, and so far everything was running smoothly. Mia made the rounds at the wine tasting tables, stopped to enjoy Lloyd in rare form as he emceed a pie eating contest, and helped one of the food vendors procure some extra Sterno cans.

Every time she was near the stage, she'd try to find a reason to linger so she could watch Cal. He actually had a small audience standing and listening to him play and it warmed Mia's heart. She'd caught snippets of his set like his impressive acoustic cover of "Red, Red Wine", but when he started to play "A Case of You", she'd stopped and listened, as did about a dozen others.

"He's really good."

Mia didn't have to turn around to see who had come up next to her. She didn't even bother to hide her admiration. There was no point with Lloyd—and truth be told, she didn't want to hide it. "He really is," she said over a warm sigh.

They stood together in silence as Cal played, his emotion coming through the song, matching the sweet and melancholy lyrics perfectly. She joined in on the polite applause and finally turned to Lloyd as she felt his eyes on her. "You know, when you started dating Tom, I remember thinking how happy I was that you'd finally found the one."

Mia's throat constricted as she regarded Lloyd. "I thought I had too," she whispered. She recalled the way she'd light up anytime she mentioned him, counting the days, hours until she could see him again.

"I see that again with you and Cal. It's different though. Like deep contentment... a settling of your soul, almost." Lloyd looked up to the sky and shook his head. "I sound like a fucking fruitcake... but you get what I mean, right?"

Mia looked back at the stage and caught eyes with Cal as

he adjusted his capo on the fretboard. His smile held a hint of surprise and something else that kept Mia rooted to the spot. He played the opening notes, and she recognized it as the first song she heard him play through the wall in her office.

Lloyd leaned over and whispered in her ear. "I think he's playing this for you."

Mia's first thought was to tell Lloyd he was being silly, but as she heard the next lyrics, she couldn't help but wonder. "Is it really this fun to have you on my mind? Is it really this cool to be in your life?"

"Mia, we need you at the wine tasting tent for a minute," Joe said as he came up to her, a slight look of panic in his eyes.

"What timing..." Lloyd stage-whispered as Mia frowned.

"Of course," she said and gave Cal one last look before heading off with her sommelier.

&

CAL TRIED TO HOLD IN A LAUGH AS THE OPENING BEATS OF "Jump Around" started after Mia announced the final round of the grape stomping competition. She clicked off the microphone and looked over at where Lloyd had commandeered the stage's sound system.

Cal stepped back so he stood shoulder to shoulder with Mia as the last two contestants stomped away while their partners held the bottle under the spigot to collect the grape juice. "You knew one way or another, Lloyd was going to get that playlist played."

Mia rolled her eyes. "At least he's keeping it clean with the lyrics. The band should be here to set up soon too, so they'll kick him off." She laughed. "You were great, by the way. I can't believe that was the first time you've played in front of a crowd."

"Thank you," he said with a shy smile and then shrugged. "I just tried to imagine I was in my room, playing for myself."

Mia regarded him for a second before she started to say something, but the crowd suddenly became raucous. They looked to see one of the contestants was close to filling their bottle, so Mia walked over to the tub and switched on her microphone to announce the winner.

Once the competition finished, Cal got to work helping clean up. He and Lloyd worked quickly while the main band set up. "Too bad Mia had to go before your last song was finished. It was really good."

Cal looked up and smiled. "Yeah, it's a cover from one of my favorite bands."

"Any reason you chose that one?" Lloyd asked with the world's worst poker face.

"I'd been working on it for a while and thought it was time to share it," Cal answered with an enigmatic smile. "Though since she was called away, perhaps I'll play it for her later."

"You really are one smooth dude," Lloyd said, shaking his head before making a show of looking around and then whispering. "Here's a tip. Mia loves to dance." With that, he walked off, whistling a barely recognizable rendition of "I Wanna Dance with Somebody."

Mia smiled as she watched the two men conversing as they moved the tubs and platforms out of the way to make room for a dance area. She wondered what they were talking about. She hoped Lloyd wasn't telling any embarrassing stories.

"We're all set, Mrs. Torwood. Gonna run a quick sound check and then we'll get started."

Mia nodded to Twisted Vines' lead singer and made her way to the other side of the stage and waited until they were done with their sound check before stepping on stage and introducing the band.

Most of the families had gone home after the pie eating contest and kids' grape stomping competition, but there was still a sizable crowd gathered to watch the band play. They were a local favorite who drew their own small legion of fans, and Mia was happy to have them play. The alcohol sales alone for the next hour would be pure profit.

Once the band started playing, Mia walked through the crowd, looking for Cal and Lloyd. She was almost all the way through the people when she caught sight of Lloyd sitting at one of the tables.

"Hey, thanks so much for your help today," she said as he pulled her into a side hug.

"Of course! You know any excuse to play at your winery and I'm here. I really do get the appeal of this lifestyle. Hard work for sure, but it's so much fun!"

"You just like the parties." Mia laughed.

"True." He shrugged. They fell quiet as they listened to the band burn through a lively rendition of "Mustang Sally". Mia felt Lloyd's eyes on her as the song ended and they applauded.

She turned to him. "What?"

"I know you want to ask me where Cal is." He smirked.

"You are taking this Cupid thing very seriously," she said, her lips edging into a smile. She wasn't going to admit that she *was* about to ask him about Cal.

"I prefer Patty Stanger," Lloyd said haughtily.

"Who?" Mia asked, brow furrowed.

Lloyd rolled his eyes. "The Millionaire Matchmaker. She has a whole show where she gets people together..."

Mia held up a hand. "Okay, I get it. Neither of us are millionaires, though." Mia said.

Lloyd leaned down and quirked an eyebrow. "The way the two of you are slaying the winery business, I'm pretty sure you'll get there."

Mia's grin came unbidden. "Yeah, we are slaying, aren't we?"

"Hell yes, Mia. I'm so damn proud of you. For a lot of reasons." Lloyd's gaze was warm and earnest, and Mia's heart filled to bursting with gratitude and affection for the man she'd known half her life. Something caught his eye, and he looked up toward the tasting room. "Now go get your boy."

Mia followed Lloyd's line of sight and smiled shyly at Cal, who had changed shirts, no doubt due to the messy clean up of the tubs. She squeezed Lloyd's hand and made her way to him, meeting him halfway, which happened to be right near where people were dancing to a classic southern rock song. "Want to dance?" Mia asked as she stood taller and leaned into Cal's ear. He nodded and smiled and took her hand.

As they clapped and moved and shimmied to the upbeat songs, Mia wondered how someone who could play music so well, could not dance. Not that she was judging Cal—far from it. She thought his silly moves and expressions were adorable. It was so attractive when someone could let loose and not take themselves too seriously.

And, boy, was she attracted to Cal. That wasn't news to her, obviously, but that night, it was hitting a different way.

An important way. The song ended to exuberant applause and Cal turned to Mia with a big, goofy smile.

"All right, folks, we're going to slow it down a bit with a classic love song. If you came with someone you love, grab 'em. If you came alone and are looking..." The singer trailed off to knowing laughter and Mia became very aware of the heat from Cal's body, close to hers, but not touching. The beginning piano notes of "(I Love You) For Sentimental Reasons" played and Mia felt Cal stiffen in surprise for a second.

"Did you ask them to play this?" Cal asked as he came around to face Mia. It was Patty and Adam's song, the one they danced to first at their wedding.

"I didn't." Mia was just as surprised as Cal. "Care to dance to it?" she asked somewhat shyly.

Cal gave her a radiant smile and reached for her hand. "I'm a much better slow dancer, I swear." He chuckled as he drew her closer. They spent the rest of the song wrapped up in their own little world, swaying slowly in the damp, trampled grass, Mia's head tilted to look into Cal's face. "I don't want to say this is a sign... but..." he said lightly to let Mia know he wasn't being serious. Mia noticed he'd been very careful not to put any kind of pressure on her and she loved him for it. *I love him.*

Her eyes widened at the revelation so much so, Cal noticed, taking it as a reaction to his statement. "Mia, I'm sorry, I didn't mean..." She put a finger to his lips and tightened her grip around his waist and laid her head against his shoulder as a tear slipped down her cheek.

22

"Let's get the rest of this cleaned up tomorrow, huh?" Mia said after she sent the rest of the permanent staff home.

"I'm certainly down with that," Lloyd said. He let out a big yawn, stretching his arms to the sky. "I'm turning in, kittens. Goodnight!" he said with a wave and turned to go inside the house without waiting for a response.

Mia chuckled and shook her head before turning to Cal. "You exhausted too?" Cal was, but if Mia asked him to stay up to watch the sunrise or go on a five-mile hike, he'd do it willingly.

"Are you?" Cal hedged before answering.

"Weirdly enough, I'm still a bit wired. I forgot to tell you, I received Patty's final journal. Megan sent it to me when I sent her back the previous one."

Cal's face lit up. "Want to read a bit tonight?"

Mia's smile was a mixture of benign embarrassment and excitement. "I do."

They headed up to the house and to no one's surprise, Lloyd was nowhere to be found. "I'll meet you on the couch in the den?" Mia asked as she gestured toward her bedroom.

"Sure. Want anything to drink?"

"No, I'm good." Mia smiled appreciatively.

He nodded and headed to the den where he turned on the light, took off his shoes, and settled in. He laid his head back and closed his eyes, thinking about the slow dance they shared. He felt something shift yet again, but he tried to temper his excitement.

This was all so new to him and he wasn't sure how to move forward. He knew he loved Mia. He remembered Mia's description of it when he'd admitted he'd never been in love. He was the damn poster child for it now. He laughed to himself at the visual that elicited.

"Hope you don't mind that I slipped into something more comfortable," Mia said, somehow appearing mischievous and innocent at the same time. She wore the men's pajama bottoms he'd seen before and a soft, white, scoop neck t-shirt. He tried not to stare.

"I don't mind at all." He managed to push past his dry throat. He wished he'd grabbed that glass of water.

Mia's lips tilted up into a smile as she settled cross-legged on the couch, knee touching Cal's thigh, the journal in her lap. She closed her eyes, opened the book, and began flipping pages at random. Cal watched her with curiosity as she stopped and placed her finger on a random page.

Cal's smile was light, inquisitive. "What are you doing?"

"Letting the universe decide what we read tonight," she said with a small smirk.

He shrugged. "I'm game."

She leaned over the book and started to read.

July 17, 1955

Today, Adam and I celebrated what we liked to call our secret anniversary. It was ten years ago to the day that he walked back into my life, a new man. That's what he likes to say. He laughs every time at his silly joke.

The last ten years have been trying, scary, joyous, triumphant. I sometimes have to pinch myself to remind me I am not in a dream. This is my life, and I'm lucky and blessed to get to live it.

When I met Adam that first summer, crop dusting for his father, I fell instantly. In those few short years when we had to hide and steal private moments, I remember thinking all I wanted to do was to be by his side. I knew he wanted that too, but there was something inside him that kept him unsettled and always searching.

I thought at first it was because of who we were and how our love was forbidden. But it turned out to be much deeper than that. It was why he left to join the WASP, despite my desperate pleas for him to stay. He literally wanted to run away from himself. We have a word for it now—Adam is a transsexual.

When he came back to me as his true self, I had a period of time where I had to adjust. I had to mourn the person I thought Adam was. But he transcended what it was to be a woman, what it meant to him to be a man. Now he is just Adam. My Adam.

I rarely think about Adam as anyone else but the man I fell in love with who survived incredible odds to return to me. Who had the courage to create the life for himself that God or whatever higher power had neglected to give him in the first place.

I love you, my darling. I'm so proud of you and honored to call you my husband.

"So, Adam was a trans man. He wasn't just a woman pretending to live as a man to make life easier for him and Patty—not that it didn't make it easier in that day and age," Cal said in wonder. He felt his connection to the vineyard deepen even more.

Mia closed the book slowly and set it on the coffee table. "May I ask you a question about transitioning?" Cal nodded. "What was it like, knowing you were in the wrong body?"

Cal thought for a few seconds about how to put it into words. He'd never really talked about it with the exception of a therapist he saw a couple of times before going on testosterone. "I hated looking in the mirror. The person looking back at me, it was a stranger. Any time I had to use the women's restroom or line up with all the other girls in class... I felt like an impostor. God, and going through puberty? I wanted to not be alive anymore." Cal shook his head slowly, remembering those years.

Mia put a hand on his knee. "I'm so glad you found a way to be yourself."

"Me too," Cal said with a self-deprecating smile. "I'm so fortunate to live in the time I do. There was a message board I found online... it saved my life. Literally. I read through every post, every reply. I found a list of doctors who were helping people get on hormone therapy. My parents, who knew how miserable I'd been, were open to the idea of me seeking professional help. I know I'm one of the few lucky ones."

"Thank goodness for that." Mia smiled and squeezed his thigh. They were silent for a few moments as Cal tried to process what was going on in his head, or rather his body as it started to respond to Mia's hand. "And now, you like your body?" Mia's tone had softened, and Cal felt his heartbeat pick up. He wasn't sure if it was out of arousal or nervousness. Most likely both.

"I do. It matches what I'd always envisioned myself to look like." Mia's hand moved just the smallest bit higher, and Cal worked to control his breathing. "Do... do you like my body?" he asked on an unsteady breath as there was no mistaking Mia's intention now. She kept staring at his lips and her eyes had become a shade darker.

"Very much so," she said, then leaned in ever so slowly. Cal met her halfway, shifting his body and sliding a hand into the hair on the back of her head. The kiss started out closed lipped, but Mia's lips quickly parted and Cal wasted no time slipping his tongue between them.

Her lips were impossibly soft and the quiet exhalation through her nose had Cal's body responding as his cock pressed against his jeans uncomfortably. They kissed like that for a few moments, bodies angled toward each other, until Mia moved to put a leg over Cal's hip. Suddenly she was straddling him with both of her hands cupping his jaw.

Her eyes were sparkling with want, not a hint of hesitation on her part. But she held herself steady and regarded Cal carefully. "I've been doing a lot of thinking and I want you to know that I really want to see where this can go—if you do too, that is."

"Are you sure?" Cal asked. He was in so deep now and needed to know if she was really all in.

"I am. I'm getting over the age difference thing, which frankly, was a real hang up for me. But if you're alright with it, I can be too. And if life has taught me anything, it is that life is too short to not take a chance on something that brings you so much joy, comfort and contentedness, pleasure...." She looked up to the ceiling, rattling words off until Cal let out an amused laugh and cupped her jaw to get her attention.

"Okay, I believe you."

"Yeah? And how about you? What are you thinking? Feeling?"

"We're on the same page. I really want to explore this with you. I just hope you can be patient with me. I've..." He closed his eyes, trying to find the right words. "I've been with a couple of women—intimately—before transitioning... but I didn't let them touch me. I've not been intimate since transitioning with anyone... except myself." Cal added with a shy grin.

Mia's expression grew serious, and she began to slide off Cal's lap. He reached for her hips and held her there. "Please, if you are comfortable, I'm more than comfortable with you—right here." He smiled and tugged her hips forward gently to emphasize his point.

She smiled, a slow, sexy one and nodded slowly. "Okay. I'll stay here." She put her hands on his chest and her eyes widened. "Wow, your heart is beating so fast."

"Yeah, well, I have a beautiful woman in pajamas sitting on my lap who I happen to really, really adore and would love to see more of."

"More of as in..." Mia started but then trailed off as one of her hands slipped to the hem of her shirt.

Cal's eyes followed her hand as he felt his erection grow even more. He knew he was too small for her to feel it through his jeans, but boy, it sure was trying to make itself known. "Only fair. You've seen me shirtless a couple of times." Without another word, Mia used her other hand and deftly pulled off her shirt leaving her naked from the waist up. "Oh," Cal said dumbly.

Mia took Cal's hands and placed them on her breasts. He gently cupped them, noting they filled his hands quite nicely. "Now you." Mia reached down and took hold of the bottom of Cal's shirt and tugged, barely letting him lean forward before she ripped it off. It got tangled up in his hands as he was very reluctant to let her breasts go.

Once they were both topless, the heat between them became sweltering. One of Cal's hands returned to Mia's breast while the other reached around her and grabbed her butt, tugging her even closer as he lifted his head to capture her lips. She moaned loudly as Cal squeezed with both hands.

"Should we take this to the bedroom," Cal whispered against Mia's open mouth.

She ground down and Cal could feel her heat. Jesus, she was going to make him cum in his pants. She pulled away and looked into his eyes and Cal could see the hesitancy in them. "Can we go to yours?"

He immediately understood why and nodded. "Of course, we can." He wrapped both arms around her lower back and slid to the end of the couch and before Mia could protest, stood smoothly. Mia let out a yelp as she wrapped her legs around his waist. "Sorry, I've always wanted to see if I could do that."

Mia wrapped her arms tightly around his neck and pressed a hot, open-mouthed kiss to his lips. "Can you walk with me like this?"

"Let's give it a try." He smiled as he took an experimental step. "Easy peasy." He smirked as he sidestepped the coffee table and headed toward the hallway before pausing. "What about our shirts?"

Mia's lips slid into a sly grin. "Leave 'em for Lloyd to find in the morning."

It took a while to get to the bedroom—Mia kept kissing Cal, and he kept bumping Mia's legs into the wall as he struggled not to get too light-headed.

Once they were inside, the door closed, Cal became self-conscious. Besides his medical team, the hired nurse for his first week post-op, and himself, no one had seen him. Mia took his hand. "We don't have to do anything you don't want to. We go at your pace, okay?"

Cal nodded and gave her a sweet smile. "Thanks. I just need a minute. Can I leave my boxers on for now?"

Mia's eyes softened. "Of course you can."

"I'll take them off in a bit... It's just that... down there..."

Mia put a hand on his chest. "I'll admit, I'm anxious to get you naked, but only when and if you feel comfortable about it. But rest assured, whatever you have going on down there, I'm going to be absolutely fine with it, okay?"

Cal covered her hand with his own and bowed his head in acknowledgment. "Can we lay down?" He just really wanted to hold Mia in that moment.

"I'd like that." Mia smiled and took his hand, leading him to the bed. As he slid in, Mia removed her pajama bottoms. Cal settled against the headboard and put his hands behind his head.

"Wait," he said as Mia put a knee down on the bed. "Let me look at you a minute." Mia's smile grew, and she took her knee off the bed and took a step back. Cal took in every inch of her—her strong legs, curved hips. She had the cutest little belly that Cal couldn't wait to kiss. "Will you turn around for me?" he asked, his voice coming out slightly raspy.

"You know, once you're comfortable, I'm having you do the same thing." She smirked as she made a slow circle.

"Of course. Turnabout is fair play." He had an idea from some of the jeans she wore that she had a nice ass. It was even better out of them. He moved to the end of the bed, sat on the edge and pulled Mia toward him.

She stepped between his legs as he wrapped his arms around her waist. He pressed his face into the soft flesh of her belly and planted warm kisses across it. He smiled against her skin when he felt her suck in a breath. He moved higher, taking a nipple into his mouth. Mia gasped.

"Sweet Jesus, that feels good. I need to lay down before I fall down." She laughed lightly.

Cal pulled away, shuffling backward and stopping near the headboard. Mia quickly followed, crawling directly on top of him, settling against him between his legs. "Is this okay?"

"More than," Cal husked out. He felt her pubic bone press against his erection and his self-consciousness was kicked to the curb. He pressed up into her and Mia gasped as her eyes widened in surprise. "I don't want to kill the mood by explaining what is down there," he said with a crooked grin. "But just know it is extremely functional and would be very, very happy to meet you."

"Yeah?" Mia beamed as she gazed into his eyes.

"Yeah," he whispered without hesitation. His heart thrummed in his chest as Mia wasted no time in pushing herself into a kneeling position. She lowered her head to plant soft, wet kisses to his chest, moving down to his sternum, stomach, belly button. When she got to the waistband of his boxers, she paused, looking up at him for permission. He nodded eagerly, desperate for her touch now.

She sat up, hooked a finger onto the band and started tugging. Cal helped by arching up and pushing the back of the boxers down. In a matter of seconds, he was completely naked. When he looked up at Mia's face for her reaction, he found her staring at his face with sweet adoration. It took his breath away.

"You're perfect, Cal. Truly."

Cal couldn't help the tear that slipped out of the corner of his eye. He'd waited so long for this moment. To be accepted and loved by another. He wiped at his eye and blew out a breath. "Sorry, to get so emotional."

Mia's eyes filled with warmth and concern. "Hey, it's

okay. Good tears, right?" Mia asked softly as she resumed her spot, lying on top of him.

He nodded. "Very good tears."

She brought a hand up to his temple, running her fingers through his hair. "Okay, well, now I just really want to make you moan. Would that be all right?"

Cal's dick twitched at the desperation in her tone and Mia glanced down to where their bodies connected. "I'll take that as a yes." She husked and began a maddeningly slow descent once again, taking her time as she trailed her lips and tongue through the soft hair that covered his stomach.

When she got to his cock, her eyes drew up to his once more, her lips quirking up into a wanton smile. Cal was crawling out of his skin with arousal. He looked down at himself, not remembering ever being that erect. It was almost painful.

He nodded and watched Mia's warm, wet lips take him in. At first contact his head slammed back into the pillow and he saw stars.

23

Mia lay next to Cal, head propped up on one hand as the other one lazily drew a path from just above his cock to his throat and back up again.

"Sorry I was such a quick trigger," Cal said with an embarrassed chuckle.

"Uh, you saw how fast I came once you put that talented tongue on me." Mia smiled coyly.

"Pot, kettle," Cal said as he turned onto his side to face Mia. "You sufficiently recovered?" he asked as he wound an arm around her waist and pulled himself closer so they were chest to chest.

"I think so." She breathed out dramatically. She wouldn't say she'd been nervous about Cal. She had prepared herself for whatever form he took—even gone as far as researching the medical steps trans men could take to become themselves.

But once they were naked and in each other's embrace, she couldn't care less what was between his legs, just as long as she could give him the attention and pleasure he deserved. Seeing how much he was aroused by her, heightened her arousal that much more and her body had taken over as her mind embraced how amazing it felt to physically connect with this man who'd been the focus of most of her thoughts the last few months. Bottom line, they were very, very compatible in the bedroom.

"Good. I want to try something, if that's okay?" Cal's smile was timid, and Mia felt her heart flutter, and her center throb.

"Sure. What did you have in mind?"

"How limber are you?" Cal asked with a sly grin.

"I've been doing yoga in some form or another for twenty years..." Her smile was coquettish.

Cal's nostrils flared, and he covered her mouth with his own, sliding his tongue against her lips until she opened them. As he deepened the kiss, he squeezed her hip and brought their pelvises together. Mia threw her leg over his hip searching for friction.

Cal pulled back, breath heavy. "Lie on your back." Mia felt a new flood of arousal at the soft command and immediately did as she was told. "Lift your knees." She did that too and Cal got between them. He pressed them slowly up until they were near her nearly to her sides. "You are limber," Cal husked as his eyes widened.

He slowly maneuvered his way on top of her, careful not to put too much pressure on the backs of her thighs. When his cock came in contact with her clit, she gasped. "Oh my God," she whispered.

Cal's eyes were closed as he pushed out a breath through his nose. "Yeah..." he croaked as he began to thrust slowly against her, gliding easily through her wet labia, to her clit and down again.

"More," Mia whispered as she canted her hips and

wrapped her arms around the back of his neck. He complied immediately, rolling his hips and pressing into her with more fervor. "Oh... fuck... it... feels... so... good..." Mia pushed out the words in time with the cadence of Cal's thrusts.

Above her, she heard Cal's breathless chuckle and pinned him with a playfully offended stare. "Are you laughing at me?"

Cal bit down on the laugh and his face contorted in pleasure. "I'm sorry, it's just... You're so fucking cute." He managed an adoring grin for only a second before his eyes closed and he started to pant.

"Slow down, tiger. You are not cumming that quick again." Mia laughed lightly as she pushed at his hips a bit with her knees. He slowed and opened his eyes, giving Mia a brilliant if not embarrassed grin.

"Sorry," he whispered, and all but stilled his hips and leaned down to kiss her deeply.

"I didn't say to stop moving," she admonished as she bucked into him.

"You are so damn bossy. I love it." He kissed her again and pulled back, his eyes glazed over with pure pleasure and contentment. "I love *you*."

It was her turn to feel a tear slip out of her eye. Cal caught it with his thumb and pressed it into his mouth. "Happy tear?" he asked softly.

"Happy tear," she confirmed with a watery smile.

"I'm gonna make you cum now. Feel free to scream my name."

Before Mia could respond, Cal rolled his hips into hers and bit down lightly on her neck. He continued his slow, hard thrusts until his name was ripped from her throat. He tumbled over quickly after her and it set off another sweet orgasm that had her pressing her face hard into his neck.

His arms were starting to shake with the effort of holding his full weight off of her and she pressed her lips into his ear. "Relax. I can take your weight."

Cal turned his head to look into her eyes. "You sure?"

She raised her head to kiss his shoulder. "I'm sure. Give me all of you," she said with a quirky grin.

"Oh, I think you just got all of me," he said cockily as he relaxed his arms. He watched her face carefully as he lowered himself all the way.

"You're heavier than you look," she said, straining her voice dramatically. His eyes widened as he started to lift off her. He was heavy, but she could take it. "I'm kidding! Come here." He settled back down, arms on either side of her head now.

She lifted her head just enough to put a kiss on the tip of his nose. She felt a stab of guilt at not returning his words of love, but she could tell he was okay with that. He knew as well as she did, those words were inevitable.

They laid there staring into each other's eyes, smiling like love-sick fools until Cal pushed into Mia once more eliciting a low moan from her. "Good news about little Cal... he can go as much and as quickly as you can."

"Let's test that out then," Mia said as she leaned up to kiss Cal. "But I want to be on top this time."

"Yes, ma'am."

PART 7: PRESS

24

Mia's eyes fluttered closed as she listened to Cal's baritone voice read from Patty's journal.

"Are you falling asleep on me?" Cal asked, amusement in his voice.

"Oh, no, just resting my eyes." They'd gone another round and had fallen asleep for about an hour but then Mia woke up, energized. She'd slipped out of the bedroom and grabbed the journal off the coffee table. When she'd returned, Cal had awoken. They had settled in, Mia's head on Cal's chest, and started at the beginning, taking turns reading.

"You sure?" Cal grinned and leaned up to plant a kiss to the top of Mia's head.

"I'm sure. Read on," Mia said, stifling a yawn.

"I'm sitting in the rocking chair in our baby's room, and I can't get enough of him. His dark hair and bright eyes. Somehow, he looks so much like Adam. All I could do was stare at him in the car as we drove home from the hospital, thinking someone would come and stop us. 'The baby of our hearts,' Adam said. I couldn't agree more."

"Do you want kids?" Mia asked before she even realized she'd spoken.

Cal's arm brushed over her head as he closed the book slowly, leaving his thumb on the page he was reading. She felt his heartbeat quicken. "Do you?" he asked.

Mia lifted her head so she could look at him. "I asked first," she said with a crooked smile, even though her heart began beating faster.

He slid the book off his lap and pursed his lips. "I... never really thought about it until recently." Mia chewed on her lip for a moment, trying to parse out Cal's answer. Was he hedging?

"Well, I'm forty-two, so I'm past my prime..." she responded, realizing she was hedging too.

Cal reached up and tucked a strand of hair behind her ear as he regarded her with a gentle, searching smile. "Do you want kids, Mia?"

"I didn't, before..." She let her sentence trail off. She'd asked the question out of the blue after having told herself for years she hadn't wanted kids. Tom hadn't had much of an opinion on the matter, so they never had a real conversation about it, then they were on the other side of their late thirties and then...

"Before?" Cal's eyebrows furrowed, clearly confused.

Truth was, she could see herself with kids with Cal. Adopted, most likely, but the idea of Cal being a father, if that's what he wanted, was very appealing. But she was getting way too ahead of herself.

"You said you hadn't thought about kids until recently? What changed?" Mia decided to turn the question back onto Cal.

"Well... you."

And there it was.

"I... that was way too soon and too much," Cal said, a look of pure chagrin on his face.

Mia rushed to respond to him, sitting up fully and crossing her legs, knees pushed into his side. "No, Cal... it's okay. I was kinda thinking the same thing. I didn't think about kids much either, but you've brought that out in me too."

"Yeah?" His smile was radiant as he pushed himself up from the headboard to sit upright as well.

"I mean... yeah. Obviously, this is very down the road stuff, but..." Mia's lips curved into a hopeful smile as they both regarded one another.

"It is, but it's good to know we are on the same page, right?"

Mia nodded vigorously. "Absolutely."

They both fell silent, their grins giddy with a hint of disbelief.

"We should probably get some sleep," Cal said after a few moments.

"We should. We still have a lot to do."

"Will you stay?" Cal asked, hope shining in his eyes.

"I'd like that."

Mia shifted herself so that she was lying in front of Cal. He stretched himself out, becoming the big spoon. Both were still naked, and Mia's body tried to respond to Cal's, but sleep was quickly winning out, also pushing away any contemplation about the conversation they'd just had. There would be time to talk and think about it all later. She brought Cal's hand up between her breasts and Cal settled his other arm under her pillow. "Comfortable?" he asked through a yawn.

"Very much," she whispered. They were both asleep in seconds.

CAL WAS KNEE DEEP IN SHOVELING GRAPE SKINS AND PULP INTO the press when he heard his phone ring. He went to the edge of the holding tank where he'd set his phone and looked at the screen. It was a call coming from the D.A.'s office so he quickly ripped off his gloves and swiped to answer it.

"Is this Cal Sanders?"

"Yes."

"This is Assistant Attorney General Clay Peters calling to let you know that a trial date has been set for Samuel Hastings."

They'd been waiting on this call. It meant charges for Samuel were going forward and Samuel would be tried for his crimes. Cal scrambled out of the holding tank, sloshing grape juice on the concrete floor. He walked to his desk, grabbed a pencil and paper, and wrote down the information Mr. Peters gave him and hung up. He pulled off his hip waders and rinsed them quickly before heading up to the house to tell Mia the good news.

MIA WAS AT THE KITCHEN TABLE LOOKING AT SOMETHING intently on her desktop when she heard a light rap on the doorframe. She looked up to see Cal a little winded but smiling. "Mr. Peters called. Trial is set for two weeks from tomorrow. They are charging him with attempted murder and arson, based on what they found at his house."

Mia sat back in her chair. She was hoping for serious charges, obviously, but... "Attempted murder?"

Cal came further into the room and sat down. "Yeah, he

couldn't go into detail, but there was evidence of his intent to take my life with that fire."

All of a sudden that terrifying moment came back to her—running down the hill after the fire trucks, seeing the lower part of the barn ablaze with Cal nowhere in sight. She leaned forward and put her elbows on the table and held her head for a moment.

Cal was right next to her before she could finish exhaling an unsteady breath. "Hey, it's okay. We're okay. He's in jail and will most likely be going away for a very long time."

Mia nodded, wiping away tears. She took a deep breath, collecting herself as she looked at Cal who was kneeling next to her, much like he had after that awful encounter with Samuel.

Had Mia been in love with Cal then? She tried to think back, to pinpoint the moment, but she couldn't. There were dozens of moments, some big, some small that built upon each other. A strong, solid foundation built on mutual respect, care, support, attraction. *Love.*

What was she waiting for? She knew what she felt when she heard Cal utter those words to her. Wasn't it time she said them too? She knew better than most how important it was to not wait to tell someone how you feel.

She regarded him, eyes wide and earnest, and laid a hand on his cheek. "I love you, Cal."

"Yeah?" His eyes shone bright, and Mia couldn't help but lean in to kiss the silly grin he had on his face.

"Yeah." She pulled back, feeling her own eyes start to fill with tears, this time happy ones. They narrowed though as she moved her hand on his cheek to the bottom of his chin. She used her forefinger and thumb to pull some grape skin off his beard. "What am I gonna do with you?"

He gave her a mischievous grin. "Anything you want."

&

MIA WATCHED THE BOTTLES MOVE THROUGH THE LINE. HER eyes tried to track one as it was filled and then moved onto the capper and then labeler. It was hypnotizing with it's repetitive, robotic motions and she liked how it soothed her mind.

She'd been teary on and off all day as they loaded case after case of bottles into the machine. Tom's first and last harvest. He should've been there with her, celebrating. But life, as it does, didn't go according to plan.

She heard Cal's voice, smiling instinctively, and looked up toward the exterior door. He waved to her as he finished up a phone call and then came over to her. His eyes were soft, his voice gentle. "How are you doing?"

He'd been so attentive and thoughtful the last couple of days as they worked on the production. Mia wanted to name it Rabbit's Foot, a funny nickname Tom had been stuck with since college. He complained about it often, but loved telling the story of how he got it.

Mia had shared it with Cal one night after they'd made love and she was surprised how at ease she was. Cal had laughed and had asked questions and by the time she'd decided that would be the name of the vintage, she'd felt a calm wash over her.

"Doing really well, actually." He came to stand in front of her and she laughed at his gentle scrutiny. "Honestly. I think the tears are just a form of release, you know? Letting go of the past, of what could have been…"

Cal had been exceedingly patient and understanding as Mia worked through the last of her grief over Tom. The guilt she felt initially had not lasted long, but there were some things she was still processing. The production of the vintage felt like a tangible end to one chapter of her life.

Now, standing right in front of her was her new chapter. One where she was so in love, and happy and hopeful. She leaned up, kissing his lips ever so softly. When he returned the kiss, just as soft, her body melted into his as her arms came up around his torso. She laid her head against his chest and sighed. "I love you, Cal. So much."

He was silent for a few seconds before she felt a kiss pressed into her temple. "I love you too, Mia. More than I can even put into words."

EPILOGUE
TWO YEARS LATER

"Babe, everything looks great. You did an amazing job," Cal said as he hugged Mia from behind.

She turned in his arms and patted his chest. "*We* did an amazing job. Thanks for setting up Lloyd's tables too." Mia smiled apologetically.

"No problem. He was in the zone making sure his debut catering event makes a good impression."

"A *great* impression," Lloyd corrected as he came up next to them. "This is my make or break. A lot of important people will be here tonight. And yes, thank you for setting up my tables, *honey*." He gave Cal a syrupy smile and planted a sloppy kiss on his cheek.

"Okay, okay." Cal laughed as he wiped his face.

"In all seriousness though, brilliant idea to have Megan's book launch here. To have it debut where the whole thing took place? Chef's kiss." Lloyd giggled at his joke. "Okay, off I go. I'll see you two later!"

Mia watched him go and shook her head. "Jury's still out on whether it was a good idea to have him open a restaurant here."

"Oh please, you couldn't have him down here fast enough." Cal laughed.

"True. He does add a bit of spice to the place. Literally."

Cal groaned at Mia's joke and pulled her in for a kiss. "How has it been two years since our first harvest together?"

"I have no idea. I'm still trying to wrap my head around it," Mia said with a crooked grin.

A lot had happened in those two years, too. Samuel had stood trial on the felony counts of arson and attempted murder, and had been found guilty on both. He was serving a thirty-year prison term.

Megan had enlisted Mia to help her write Patty and Adam's story, and their manuscript had gotten picked up for publication. Early reviews were glowing with praise.

Cal had moved back into his apartment after it was repaired for about a year until Mia whined that she missed waking up to him every morning, even though he stayed over most nights. Lloyd, who was now officially splitting time between Feast in San Francisco and Wine and Dine at the winery was quick to snap up the furnished apartment. Cal had even left the *Kill Bill* poster for him.

The winery had continued to expand its features, now hosting weddings and other special events, winemaking classes, and exclusive tours. As Cal had predicted their goat rental business was a huge success. He'd had a steady stream of current and prospective vineyard owners come through, looking for advice on implementing biodynamic farming techniques.

"But they've been a good two years, huh?" Cal asked with a crooked smile.

"The best, sweetheart." She leaned up to give him a quick kiss and then patted his butt lightly. "Guests start arriving soon. We better get back to work."

Cal beamed as he watched Mia make her way to the stage after Megan's reading. It had been a no-brainer to tie in their first vintage together with Patty and Adam's story, but it had been really hard to keep it a secret from Megan and her family.

"Megan, we've really enjoyed getting to know you and your family and its extraordinary history over the last two years. We were so honored to be a part of the making of this book."

Cal almost missed his cue; he was so excited. He smiled sheepishly and jogged the few feet to the front of the stage to hand Mia the bottle of wine. She smiled her thanks and turned to Megan. "To commemorate this day and the amazing love story of Patty and Adam, we wanted to dedicate a vintage to them. Howe's Oak 2022."

The crowd erupted into applause as Mia presented the bottle to Megan who immediately began tearing up as she accepted the bottle.

"Beautiful gesture," Lloyd said, and Cal was surprised to see a look of wistfulness on the man's face. "You're being summoned." Lloyd pointed to the stage and Cal saw Mia waving him up. Before he could make a move, Lloyd caught his arm. "You aren't doing it right here, are you?"

Cal shook his head. "Nah, I have something a little more intimate planned."

Lloyd gave him an approving smile. "You really do know our girl, don't you?"

"Yeah, but I like to think I'm still learning more about her every day."

"Want to go for a walk with me?" Cal asked Mia as she finished tipping the last of the waitstaff.

"Sure," Mia said, exhausted, but exhilarated still from how well the book launch and vintage name announcement went.

They walked in silence, Mia content to let Cal lead the way. It wasn't long before she realized where they were headed. She was surprised to see a blanket and some string lights adorning the old oak tree, though. "Cal..." Mia breathed.

"I just wanted to do a little something for you to show you how much I appreciate you." He walked ahead of her and straightened a corner of the blanket that had been turned up by the breeze. "Come, sit."

She lowered herself to the blanket and watched as he took an already open bottle of wine out of an empty ice bucket. "Is that the Howe's Oak?" Her eyebrows rose in delighted surprise.

"Of course," Cal said as he poured a couple of ounces into stemless glasses. They had already sampled the vintage, as had a handful of their sommelier friends, and they all agreed it would be a sought after wine for years to come.

Mia took her glass and swirled it around, marveling at its deep, dark purple hue. She brought it to her nose and closed her eyes, taking in the spicy notes of pepper mixed with bold, luscious, dark berries. She took a healthy mouthful, swishing it around as the taste of black cherries, vanilla, spice, and smoke exploded on her tongue.

"I've never been jealous of a glass of wine before," Cal quipped causing Mia to open her eyes and look at him with mild embarrassment. She quickly recovered though and gave him a sultry look.

"Well, you did make the wine that's having its way with my mouth."

Cal's amused grin fell as his eyes darkened. Without taking his eyes off Mia's, he took a sip of his own wine, set it down and crawled over to her on all fours until he had her back pinned against the tree trunk. He removed the glass from her hand and pressed his lips to hers. When she opened them, she was surprised as warm, sweet liquid rushed into her mouth. She swallowed and opened her mouth more, drinking him in, heedless to the few drops spilling from her bottom lip. He pulled away much sooner than Mia would have liked, leaving her chasing his kiss.

"God, you drive me crazy," Cal said as he settled in next to her. Mia, whose libido had just been jumpstarted, moved to straddle his hips. They made out for a few more minutes before Cal pulled away again. "Will you do something for me?"

"Anything..." she said dreamily.

He leaned up and reached for something on the blanket, bringing it up to his chest and hiding it from her view. "I planned on getting down on one knee, but honestly, this is better..."

She blinked a few times, trying to comprehend what he was saying and when it hit her, tears gathered in the corner of her eyes. "Mia, will you do me the honor of letting me be your partner in life?"

She threw her arms around his neck and crushed him and whatever he was holding against her chest.

"I guess that's a yes?" She heard his muffled words and loosened her grip, but only a fraction.

"It is," she whispered and leaned in, kissing him with fierce intensity. When she pulled away, it was his turn to look dazed.

"Oh, uh, you want to see the ring?" He smiled dopily and opened his hand to reveal a beautiful platinum band with a small, round diamond. It was elegant and understated, exactly what Mia liked.

"Put it on?" Mia asked as she brought her left hand between them, and Cal slipped the ring on.

"Perfect fit." Cal beamed. "Want to celebrate right here, under the stars?" Cal asked as his hands reached around to caress Mia's butt.

"I thought you'd never ask," Mia purred. Cal smirked and shifted under Mia but stopped abruptly and furrowed his brow. "What's wrong?"

"Something is under the blanket." Mia slipped off his lap, and he moved the blanket. "Huh..."

"What is it?" Mia asked, peering over his shoulder.

"It's a half-buried bottle, looks like." He dug around it for a few minutes, finally freeing what looked to be a wine bottle from the packed soil. "Still intact with the cork and everything." He lifted it to the light and examined it.

"There's something inside it," Mia said excitedly, their impending celebration momentarily forgotten. Cal pulled the cork, which pretty much crumbled away in his fingers. He turned the bottle upside down and a rolled piece of paper fell out. Mia quickly picked it up and unraveled it. She held it up to the light and her eyes widened. "It looks like a page from Patty's journal. It's dated August 17, 1976."

"A month after Adam died," Cal recalled. "Can you read it?"

"Yeah," Mia said, squinting under the low string lights.

When you asked me how I fell in love with someone like you, I'd have to start with the first time I saw you. You jumped off the wing of your father's plane, declaring to my father you were fit to do the job and if he didn't like it, he could go hire the drunk fella down the road.

You had a fierceness that came from somewhere deep inside you. That fierceness showed itself in so many different ways: how you did your job, how you fought injustice, how you'd take me in your arms and tell me nothing would keep us apart.

And when it did, for a time, you came back to me. Against all odds and in a different form, but it was you, my beloved. It was you who found a way to honor your promise and together we built a life that went beyond my wildest dreams.

So, when you asked how I could love someone like you, I say to you, how could I not? Love, if it is the true kind, transcends all barriers, whether they be of the mind or the body. Whether they be from within or external.

Being in love with you was the easiest thing I've ever done.

Please wait for me the way I waited for you all those years ago. I'll be home with you soon, my dearest Adam.

"Oh, wow," Cal said.

"Yeah," Mia said as she wiped away a tear. She gently rolled the paper back up and slipped it into the bottle.

"We'll get a new cork for it and just put it back where we found it?" Mia nodded, still a bit shaken by the find. "You okay?" Cal asked gently, rubbing Mia's back.

"Yeah... it's just kind of..." She trailed off, words failing her at the moment. She didn't want to get caught up in the reminder of loss. So, she'd take it as a message from Patty. Let her love transcend fear. She turned fully to face Cal, putting a hand on his cheek. "Being in love with you is the easiest thing I've ever done, too."

Cal's eyes brightened. "Yeah? Even when I snore and leave my dirty socks everywhere?"

Mia laughed. "Even then." She leaned in, kissing him softly. She was about to try to restart the flame that had begun earlier when she heard her phone ring. "Ignore it," she mumbled against his lips. She pushed him down to the blanket as the call went to voicemail. They both groaned in frustration when Cal's phone started ringing.

"Someone really wants to get ahold of us." He sighed as he dug his phone out of his back pocket. His eyes shot up to Mia's when he looked at the caller ID.

"It's Beth."

"Answer it!" Mia all but shrieked as Cal fumbled to accept the call.

"Hi, Beth," Cal said somewhat breathlessly. "Yes, she's right here... We're alone..." Mia narrowed her eyes at him impatiently as he hit the speaker button.

"Hey, you two, I have some news. Ryan's back in care... we're now looking for permanent placement."

"You mean adoption?" Mia asked, trying to temper her excitement. They'd had the sweet thirteen-year-old transgender boy for six months before his grandparents said they'd take custody, leaving both of them—as well as Ryan—heartbroken.

"Yes. Adoption. I'm sure I don't even need to ask, but you two are still interested, right?"

Mia put her hand over her mouth, trying to hold back a sob as she nodded vigorously. Cal reached out a hand and she grabbed it, squeezing it hard.

"Yes, Beth. Absolutely."

A FAVOR...

If you enjoyed this book, please review on Amazon, Goodreads, or where ever your preferred review site is. There aren't a lot of books with a trans man/cis woman pairing and I'd love it if this book could reach as many people as possible looking for representation. Thank you for reading!

ABOUT THE AUTHOR

L. Dreamer is a part-time van lifer and full-time wanderer. If he isn't out mountain biking, kayaking or hiking, he's in his writing shed working on his next queer romance.

Check out Dreamer's website and join his mailing list if that's your thing.

Luc Dreamer

ALSO BY L. DREAMER

Heart of Gold

Heart Sings

In the Black

The Burden of Happiness

'Tis the Season

The One to Walk Away